RANDOM
HOUSE

LARGE
PRINT

FROM THE LISTENING HILLS

FROM THE LISTENING HILLS

LOUIS L'AMOUR

RANDOM HOUSE
LARGE PRINT

1811 1904
N

Copyright © 2003 by Louis and
Katherine L'Amour Trust

All rights reserved under International and
Pan-American Copyright Conventions.
Published in the United States of America
by Random House Large Print in
association with Bantam Books, New York
and simultaneously in Canada by
Random House of Canada Limited, Toronto.
Distributed by Random House, Inc., New York.

*The Library of Congress has established a
Cataloging-in-Publication record for this title.*

0-375-43211-6

www.randomlargeprint.com

FIRST LARGE PRINT EDITION

10   9   8   7   6   5   4   3   2   1

This Large Print edition published in accord
with the standards of the N.A.V.H.

CONTENTS

FROM THE LISTENING HILLS

SAND TRAP

Before he became fully conscious he heard the woman's voice and some sixth sense of warning held him motionless. Her voice was sharp, impatient. "Just start the fire and let's get out of here!"

"Why leave that money on him? It will just burn up."

"Don't be such an idiot!" her voice shrilled. "The police test ashes and they could tell whether there was money or not . . . don't look at me like that! It has to look like a robbery."

"I don't like this, Paula."

"Oh, don't be a fool! Now start the fire and come on!"

"All right."

Monte Jackson held himself perfectly still. Despite the pounding in his skull he knew what was happening now. They believed him dead or unconscious and, for some reason, planned to burn the house and him with it.

From some distance away he heard footsteps and then a door closed. All was quiet except for the ticking of a clock. Returning consciousness brought with it pain, a heavy, swollen pain in the back of his head. He opened his eyes and saw linoleum, turquoise and black squares, an edge of enameled metal and beyond it, lying against the wall in what he now realized was the dark corner behind a washing machine, a man's dress sock, lightly covered with dust. His head hurt, it hurt badly and he wasn't sure he could move.

His fingers twitched . . . okay, movement was possible. He didn't get up, but he thought about it . . . were they gone? Who were *they*? A woman. He could almost remember her, something . . .

He smelled smoke. Smoke! And not wood smoke either, burning plastic, amongst other things. He was definitely going to have to get up.

He lurched to his knees, sending a flurry of twenty- and one-hundred-dollar bills to the floor; his head swam and black spots passed before his eyes. He was in the utility room of a house somewhere, flames crackled, there was money everywhere. He grabbed the side of the washing machine and stood up, a haze of smoke hung in the doorway before him, he stumbled forward into a kitchen. Behind him there was a good two thousand dollars in currency scattered on the floor . . . but other things had his attention.

The pain and the increase in light blurred his vision. A roll of paper towels, conveniently placed near a burner on the gas range, was spreading fire to items left on the counter, brown paper bags from the market, a wooden box built to hold milk bottles, and from there to the gaily colored drapes over the sink . . . one whole side of the room was in flames. On the floor lay a man in his shirtsleeves and wearing an apron, a caked reddish-brown stain on his side. Beside him lay two items. A small pistol and a heavy, cast-iron pan.

Monte Jackson suddenly had a vision of that pan coming down on the side of his head. It was only then that he noticed the food that was splattered all over his right shoulder and sleeve. He touched his scalp and nearly lost his balance. It was split, split to the bone.

He turned, and as the lightbulb over the sink burst from the heat of the fire, staggered to a door that looked like it opened onto a side yard; he yanked at the knob. It turned but the door wouldn't open, it just rattled in the jamb. A lock? The heat was like the broiling desert sun and growing even more intense. The lock needed a key . . . and the key was not in it.

As the paint began to blister on the wall next to him, Monte Jackson dropped to all-fours and crawled into the burning kitchen, desperately headed for the door that he assumed led to the dining room. He slipped in the sauce that covered the floor near the body, his hand hit the pistol and it went skittering into a corner. He pushed through the swinging door and he was suddenly in the comparative calm of a butler's pantry.

Shadows thrown by the flames fled ahead of Jackson as he scrambled to his feet and ran down the hallway. Past the dining room, the living room, then the front door was before him. He slid to a stop; a faint whistling sound came from under the door . . . air rushing into the house, feeding the fire that was spreading in the kitchen and licking its way down the ceiling of the hallway. He could feel its heat at his back. Jackson turned the knob and pulled the door open. It came easily, like one of those automatic doors in a supermarket, the pressure of the outside air pushing it inward. The fire roared to greater life behind him, flames pouring up the stairwell and into the second floor.

Jackson stumbled across a wide front porch and down a short set of concrete steps, the free warm air of the summer night enfolding him. He swayed on his feet. What was going on? He remembered a building with arches along the sidewalk, sitting in a bar, a girl . . .

Riverside. He was in Riverside. He had been in the bar at the Mission Inn!

Fire lit the second-floor windows of the house. He had to call the fire department . . . but, what of the man on the floor? The man was dead. The man was dead and he probably owned the house that was burning. Monte Jackson wanted to be far away. Far away in a place where none of this could have happened.

Headlights swung into the front yard and Jackson turned. But the car was not coming in from the road, it had been parked behind the house, near the detached garage.

"It's him! You idiot, get him!" He heard the woman's harsh voice again, and suddenly the car accelerated. Jackson backed up, turned, then ran. The dark sedan sprayed gravel as a heavy foot was applied to the gas. He dodged, jumped a hedge and went to his knees, but was up with a lunge and into the shrubbery, slamming blindly into a woven wire fence, hitting it hard enough to throw him back, he ploughed on. The car ground to a stop, caught in the hedge, and he heard the doors pop open. There was a shot. He felt the hot breath of the bullet pass his cheek. He crouched and ran, sighted a gate . . . how he got through it and into the orchard beyond he never knew.

Twice he stumbled and fell headlong, but forced himself to keep running until he was completely out of breath.

As his head cleared he caught the sound of tires as a car drove by on gravel. Following the sound, he emerged from the brush on the lip of a ravine dividing the wood from a county road.

It was not a main road but, by the look of it, plenty of cars were passing. If he could get a lift, get out of here, well, maybe he could figure out what happened.

He thought of his appearance and lifting a fumbling hand, felt gingerly of the wound along his scalp. There was dried blood in his hair and on his cheek and ear.

The sound of water led him to an irrigation ditch where he dropped to his knees and bathed the blood away, then dried himself with his shirt and handkerchief. Carefully, he combed hair over the wound to try to conceal it. Behind him, the orchard was silhouetted against the glowing cloud of smoke that rose from the fire.

So what had happened? Well, there was the lounge at the Mission Inn. A girl, pretty enough . . . pretty enough for a man who had spent the last three months in the desert. He had caught her eye momentarily, but what would a girl like that want with him?

Unfortunately, it was all coming back to him.

The girl, woman, (he had other names for her now) . . . had been well dressed but was obviously nervous. A man, a big young man, was hanging around the bar, watching her. The two never spoke but Monte Jackson hadn't been in the desert so long that he was blind; the man didn't want to be noticed, but he was watching the woman whose name, Jackson now knew, was Paula.

He had finished his drink and left the

bar, there was no time in his life right now for women; few women would tolerate the way he was living. There was also no time in his life for whatever kind of drama was brewing between her and the man at the bar. He had no time for it, but when the dark sedan had pulled up beside him as he walked down the street, he had found himself involved, regardless.

After cleaning up, he decided against trying to get a ride. Although he was hurt, a minor concussion, at least, a torn scalp, bruises and scrapes from his escape, and a nasty cough from the smoke he had inhaled, he had to think, and he was still sure that his appearance, especially so close to a fire, would draw unwanted attention.

His memories were sorting themselves out and he thought he knew where he was. A little farm, a nice gentlemanly farm, on the outskirts of Riverside. He turned right and started walking along the road. Occasionally cars sped past. At first he ducked into the ditch when he saw them coming, fearing a bullet from Paula or her friend. But soon after he started out he had heard fire engines in the distance, probably on a parallel road, and figured that Paula might be busier trying to explain to the cops and the fire crew what had happened than she was trying to find him. So he walked along the shoulder of the road, squinting against the dust of passing cars, until he came to an intersection. The new road was paved, and on the other side, under a streetlamp, was an empty bus stop.

The bus got him within a block of the El Mirage Motel where, earlier in the day, he had taken a room on the second floor. He no longer had his key but the desk clerk remembered him and gave him another. The room was as he had left it just hours before. He went to the bathroom and washed his face and scalp again. Though very painful, he cleaned the wound, and that started it bleeding again. He tore strips from a towel and bound it up as best he could, the kind of pressure it needed was impossible, for the bruising was worse than the cut. He slipped out of his torn and filthy clothes and noticed that the pockets were almost empty . . . it was not only his room key that was gone, his wallet was missing too! He sat down next to the telephone. He should call the police.

That was simple. That was the right thing to do. And what would he tell them? Well, the truth; a woman had picked him up in her car as he left the lounge at the Mission Inn. She had said that a man was following her and that she would like him to see her home. Her husband, a local doctor, would then drive him wherever he wanted to go.

It had made sense at the time.

Once at the farm, she had asked if he wanted a drink. When he said yes, she'd suggested that he get a coaster out of the cabinet behind him. He had turned, and when he had turned back, the big man from the bar had been standing there and had hit him on the head with the cast-iron pan. He'd fallen to his knees and the man had hit him again. The last thing that he remembered was the woman, Paula, fitting his hand around a small automatic pistol . . . curling his fingers around it, then carrying it away in a handkerchief.

He was a patsy. The two had set him up but it hadn't worked. He definitely should call the police.

Except that thought worried him. With his wallet gone he had no ID. No one knew him here; the year or so since leaving the service he had spent prospecting in the desert. His terminal leave pay and what he had saved financed the venture, for his expenses had been small. He'd never had an address or a job anywhere except for the Army and he'd only gone there because a judge had given him a choice, the military . . . or jail.

He had a record, that could be a problem. Breaking and entering with a gang of other kids from Tempe. His uncle, an old jackass prospector, had taken a strap to him many a time but it hadn't helped. The Army had and after eight years in a ranger company he had emerged a different man.

None of which was going to help him now. He had escaped but the woman was going to have a lot of explaining to do and he was suddenly certain of what she was going to say. The very story she had tried to set up in the first place would be her best bet now. Someone had tried to rob the dead man in the house (was it her husband?), the house had caught fire just as she was returning home. He didn't know exactly how she'd spin it but he had no doubt that she would identify him as the killer . . . and she probably had his wallet.

He felt short of breath and his throat was tight. Everything he had learned in the Army told him to call the police. But his childhood, the poor kid raised in an ovenlike trailer who had been chased by the cops down dusty alleys and through weed-grown scrap yards, said something else. The world he lived in now was not the world of the military. He could not count on officials being the hard but fair officers he had once known. He could not count on those around him to take responsibility for their actions or to take pride in their honesty.

In the end he split the difference. Quickly dressing in clean clothes, he packed his bag and, using a stash of money left in his shaving kit, paid the bill. He gingerly pulled his hat on over the makeshift bandage and set out for the bus station.

After buying his ticket he turned to a phone booth and, pulling the door shut, dropped a dime in the slot. After speaking with an operator and holding for a minute or so a voice responded. "Robbery-Homicide, Lieutenant Ragan speaking."

Jackson took a deep breath. "Lieutenant Ragan, don't think this is a crank call. I'm going to outline a case for you. Listen. . . ."

Without mentioning his name he outlined his story from the moment he'd been accosted by the woman on the street. He told how he was lured into her home, that he'd been knocked out, and the plans to fire the house. He ended suddenly. "Ragan, I need help. This man, whoever he was, was killed, shot, and these people are looking for a cover story . . . something that doesn't implicate them. I'm not a killer, but you can see the spot I'm in, can't you?"

"I guess so," the policeman said. "What do you want from me?"

"Look into it from my angle, don't just believe everything you're told."

"We never just believe what we're told." Ragan's voice was dry, nearly expressionless. "Look, it's not my case. All I can tell you to do is to give yourself up. Just come in and let us do our job."

Monte Jackson hung the receiver gently on the hook.

He had done what he could. Once on his claim, it might be months, even years before they found him. But he knew too much to believe he could escape forever.

Yet he must have breathing space. He was in a trap, but if he had time he might think his way out or perhaps, the investigation would turn up something that led away from him. He had made an attempt to offer an element of doubt. The police might accept the woman's story, yet if they had cause to look further, what might they find?

They were calling his bus, and in a minute he was moving with the line, then boarding the bus north to Inyokern. Fortunately, it was soon moving.

When the bus stopped at Adelanto he glanced out the window and saw someone who gave him an idea. "Hey, Jack!" he called. "How far you going?"

"Bishop," he said, walking toward Monte. "Why?"

"Look," Monte explained. "I've got to call L.A. and I've got to leave the bus here. No use to waste my ticket, so you might as well take it and ride to Inyokern, then buy one on from there."

The fellow hesitated briefly. "Sure thing. What do you want for it?"

"Don't worry about it," Jackson said, turning away quickly. Now the bus driver would never realize he had lost a passenger, and if the ticket was traced it would have been used to Inyokern.

He was a tall young man with broad shoulders and he had always walked a lot. Fortunately, the morning was cool. If he remembered correctly it was seven miles to Oro Grande on Highway 66. He started out, walking fast along the intersecting road. Yet he was in luck, for when he had gone scarcely a mile a pickup slowed and the door opened. He got in.

"Goin' far?" He was a dark-haired man in boots and Levi's.

"Oro Grande, to catch a bus for Barstow."

"Lucky," the fellow grinned, "I'm drivin' to Barstow. On to Dagget, in fact, if you care to ride that far."

At Dagget, Jackson walked over the connecting road to Yermo and waited four hours for the bus for Baker. Arriving in Baker he walked through town to the little house owned by Slim Garner, who worked the neighboring claim over in Marble Canyon. He found Slim watering his rough patch of lawn.

"Hey, Monte! Didn't think to see you here."

"Are you headed back to Death Valley? I could use a ride."

"Sure, no problem." He turned off the hose, looking around at the yard, which was mostly dirt. "I'm not here enough to grow weeds, I should give up and save the water. Put your haversack in the truck, I'll load up and we'll go."

Slim's Powerwagon ground northward and a hot wind blustered in through the open windows. Jackson dozed in the passenger seat, trying to get some rest, although the shaking of the truck made his head throb. The radio played old songs through a speaker that was stuck to the top of the dash by the magnet in its base, the two wires connecting it running down into the defroster vent.

When the news came on, however,

Monte Jackson found himself coming fully awake.

"In Riverside, a prominent doctor was killed last night. Martin Burgess was shot to death in an apparent robbery attempt and his house caught fire and burned either as a complication of the struggle or in an attempt to cover up the crime. The doctor's wife, Paula Burgess, was returning home and saw a man flee from the burning house. The assailant is still at large."

The news continued. There was a war going on in Indochina and a scandal brewing in the L.A. City Hall, the weather was expected to be hot and get hotter.

"We'll be workin' nights this week," Slim groused.

"What?" Jackson made believe he'd just woken up.

"Gonna be hot!"
"Yeah? So what else is new?"

Leaving Garner in Marble Canyon, Monte Jackson hiked west in the long summer twilight. His claim was near Harris Hill and coming from Slim's place was the back way in. That was good given everything that was going on right now, he thought. He wanted to have a chance to look over the site and confirm that no one was there ahead of him. If he was going to have a sit-down with the authorities, he wanted to walk into a police station under his own power like an innocent man, not be arrested, like a fugitive.

But as the light faded from the sky he could see that his cabin was undisturbed. And for about forty-eight hours, his life returned to normal.

• • •

That night he slept long and deep, a needed escape from all that had happened. The next day he carefully cleaned the wound again, this time properly, with peroxide, and then bandaged it. He noticed, while looking in the mirror, that the pupil of his left eye was noticeably larger than the right . . . he'd been right, the man who'd hit him had given him a concussion. He puttered around the house that day doing small chores and cleaning up. He also repacked his haversack with some food and a canteen, and then cleaned his rifle, an old Savage Model 99 that had belonged to his uncle.

On the second day Monte Jackson walked up to the diggings. He wore his sunglasses until he was inside the tunnel, and that seemed to help his head a bit.

At the end of his drift he picked up a drill steel and, inserting it into the hole, started to work, yet after only a few blows with the single jack his head began aching with a heavy, dull throb, and he knew that the scalp wound had taken more out of him than he had believed.

Leaving his tools in the drift, he picked up his canteen and shirt and started back to the cabin, yet he had taken no more than a dozen steps before he heard a car. It was, he knew, still some distance off, rumbling and growling along the rough road that came in from the west. Having listened to other cars on that road he knew approximately where it would be, and he knew that before it could reach his cabin it must go south at least two miles, then back north. It was the merest trail, and the last of it uphill.

He was no more than a minute climbing the sixty feet to the crest. Lying on his stomach, he inched the last few feet and scanned the trail. It was a utility wagon, the kind that was available for rent in Bishop for day trips into the Sierras, and in it were two people.

Jackson squirmed swiftly back, then arose and started at a trot for the drift. Once inside the tunnel he caught up a few handfuls of dust and dropped them from above so that they would filter down over his tools and the spot where he had worked to give an appearance that would lead them to believe he had not recently used them. Hurrying to his cabin he gathered his things, padlocked the door, and then paused to listen. There was no sound.

That meant they had left the vehicle at the spring and were coming on foot. Keeping to rocks and gravel, he went down into the arroyo and crossed it, cutting over to enter a deep gash in the hill. Then coming out of the small canyon he climbed to the crest overlooking his cabin.

After about twenty minutes he saw them coming. It was Paula and the big blond man. The man walked slightly in advance, and had an automatic pistol tucked into the waistband of his pants. Monte settled down to watch and, despite the pain in his head, was amused to find himself enjoying it. That they had come to kill him he had no reason to doubt, yet as he watched their cautious approach he found himself with a new idea.

He was the one man who actually knew Paula Burgess guilty of murder, yet by coming here they had delivered themselves into his hands. This was his native habitat. He knew the desert and they did not. Their jeep was the tenuous link to the world they knew, and if anything happened to that vehicle they were trapped.

Their incompetence was obvious from their movements. Once the man stepped on a stone that rolled under his foot, causing him to fall heavily. He caught himself on his hands, but had Monte been in the cabin he would have heard it. They looked at the lock, then peered in the windows. Certainly, no one was in the shack with a padlock on the door. After a few minutes of conversation the man started toward the drift. Paula Burgess remained alone before the cabin.

Monte Jackson stared at her with rising anger. She had chosen him for killing exactly as she might have chosen a certain fly for swatting. Now they were here, hunting him down like an animal.

He had his rifle and he could kill them both easily. For a man who had made Expert with a half-dozen weapons, two hundred yards was nothing, yet shooting was unnecessary. Of their own volition they had come into the desert but, he vowed, they would leave only when he willed it.

Sliding back from the ridge he got up and walked fast, then trotted a short distance. The sun was high and it was hot now, but he must get there first, and must have a little time.

•   •   •

The jeep stood near the spring. Squirming under it, he opened his clasp knife and, using a carefully chosen rock as a hammer, he punched a hole in the side of the gas tank. The fuel spurted out and, working the knife blade back and forth, he enlarged the hole. Given the angle of the vehicle and positioning of his hole he figured that no more than two gallons would soon remain in the tank and if this was like the trucks that he had used in the Army, the last half gallon might well be useless. He worried that they might see or smell the drained fuel but it was over one hundred degrees and there was no humidity, so the gas would evaporate quickly. He scattered several handfuls of sand over the widening stain to help out. Then he flattened out behind some creosote brush about twenty yards from the jeep, and waited.

•   •   •

They came down the path, the woman complaining. "He's got to be around somewhere, Ash! He has to hide, and where is there a better place?"

"Well he's not here now! It was a fool idea. Let's just sit tight and wait for that insurance!" Ash shook his head. "Let him stay here and rot . . . they'd never believe him, anyway! If anybody knew we were up here it would look suspicious."

"Oh, shut up! I started this and I want to finish it!" Paula got into the jeep. Her blouse was damp on the shoulder blades and armpits and the two-mile walk had done neither of them any good. She was in heels, and he wore tight city shoes. They were good and hot now, and dry.

"I'm going to get a drink," Ash said, "it's a long ride back."

"Come on! We can stop by that last place for a Coke! I thought you wanted to get out of here?"

Ash got in and the jeep started willingly

enough. When they had gone Monte Jackson got up. He took his time for there was lots of it, he knew about how far they would be able to get. He made up a few sandwiches, put them in the haversack with a blanket and his leather jacket, then stuffed cookies into his pockets and with his rifle and canteen, walked east, away from the road.

From time to time he stopped and mopped sweat from his brow, and then walked on toward Marble Canyon. They would make anywhere from five to ten miles with the gas they had, traveling in low as they would. It was only six miles to Dodd's Spring but he doubted if they would get so far.

Slim Garner was washing dishes when Jackson showed up. "Too late for coffee," he said.

"Not hungry, Slim." He grounded his

rifle. Garner glanced curiously at the pack and rifle but said nothing. "Tell you what you might do, though. About the day after tomorrow you might drive over to Stovepipe Wells and call the sheriff. Ask him to meet me at Dodd's Spring and to bring Ragan from the Riverside Police Department. Robbery-Homicide. You tell him it's the Burgess case."

Garner stared. "Homicide? That's murder!"

"You're darn' tootin', it is! Call him, will you?"

"You ain't fixin' to kill nobody?" Slim protested.

"No, the fact is I'm takin' a gamble to prove I haven't killed somebody already." Knowing he must not walk again until the cool of the evening, he sat down and quietly spun his yarn out while Slim listened. Garner nodded from time to time.

"So they come up here after you?" Slim asked. He chuckled, his old eyes twinkling. "Sure, I'd like to see their faces when they find they are out of gas clean over there on the edge of the Valley!"

"Do you suppose they could find Dodd's Spring?"

"Doubt it. Ain't so easy lest you know it's there." He grinned. "Let 'em sweat for a while. Do 'em good: Make 'em feel talkative."

Dusk was settling over the desert when Monte Jackson again saw the utility wagon. Evidently gas had not been their only trouble, for a punctured tire was now lying in the backseat. The jeep was stopped on open ground and the man and woman stood beside it, arguing. Their gestures were plain enough, but when he crawled nearer, he could hear them.

"Why not start tonight? We've got to have gas and you could be there by morning."

"Are you crazy? It's twenty miles, and maybe thirty!"

"Well, what if it is?" she asked irritably.

"In this country, wearing these shoes, I'd be lucky to make it in two days! And without water? What do you think I am?"

"What a guy!" she exclaimed contemptuously. "You let me plan it all, do everything, and then you come off without enough gas to get us back!"

"Look, honey," he protested patiently, "we had enough gas. There should be seven or eight gallons left! He dropped to his knees and peered under the rear of the vehicle. "There's a hole," he said.

"A hole?"

"He put a hole in our tank . . . or someone did."

"What do you think he intends to do?"

"Do?" Ash shrugged. "I don't know, maybe call the cops. I'm more worried about us!"

"What do you mean?"

"We're in the middle of the desert. Nobody comes out here. We could die, okay." He sucked in a deep breath. "You're worried about the guy being a witness. You're worried about the cops. I'm worried about the fact that we're in the desert and, unless it was a rock that put a hole in our tank, this guy Jackson is the only person who knows we're here."

"So what do we do?"

"We'd better wait. Cars have been over this trail, and one might come along. If none does, then I can start walking by daylight. At night I couldn't keep to the trail."

There is no calm like the calm of a desert at dusk, there is no emptiness so vast, no silence so utterly still. Far, serrated ridges changed from purple to black, and the buttes and pinnacles pointed fingers of shadow into the wasteland. Stars were coming out, and the air grew faintly chill. Monte Jackson pulled on his coat and crawled closer . . . it was time to have a little fun.

"I'll build a fire," Ash said.

"Don't pick up a snake," Monte said.

The woman gave a little shriek, but though their eyes lifted, they were looking some distance off to his left where a rock cliff had caught the sound and turned it back to them. Ash put a hand on his gun but kept it under his shirt. When there was no other sound they moved together and stood there, looking up toward the ridge where he lay, a long low ridge of sand and rock.

"Who's there?" the man called out.

Jackson settled back against a warm rock, and waited. A tall saguaro, one of those weird exclamation points of the desert, stood off to his left, and beyond it the desert stretched away, a place of strange, far beauty, and haunting distance. A coyote broke the silence suddenly, yapping at the moon, the sound chattering plaintively against echoing cliffs until the long valley resounded with it, and then it ceased suddenly, leaving a crystalline silence.

He heard a stick cracking then and saw a flashlight moving along the ground, then more breaking sticks.

Monte turned his face toward the cliff and asked, "What about water?"

Ash peered around him in the gathering dark. "Hey you! We're in trouble, we need help!"

"Trouble?" Monte said. "No. You're not in as much trouble as you're gonna be!"

There was a brief, whispered conversation. Then . . .

"Now see here," the man blustered, "you come down! Come down and we'll talk about this."

Monte Jackson did not reply. The fire would help with the cold but it would not help their thirst. By noon tomorrow they would be suffering. They asked for it, and a little fear is a wholesome thing.

•   •   •

Leaving his position, Monte hiked up the wash to the spring. He ate a sand-wich, had a long drink, chewed a salt tablet and settled down for the night. Awakening with the first dawning light he made coffee, ate another sandwich, and then returned before full sunup to his vantage point. The two were huddled in the jeep. But now the day was warming up, from a nighttime low in the mid-fifties, today it would be over one hun-dred degrees.

"It'll be over a hundred today," he called loudly. "Without water, you might last from one to three days. If you are very lucky you could make twenty miles."

Ash got out of the jeep. "Wait a minute!" he called. "I want to talk to you!" His voice tried to be pleasant, but starting toward the rocks he slipped his hand behind his back, reaching for the gun. Knowing how difficult it is to see a man who does not move, Monte lay still on the dusty ground.

Ash got close to the rocks, then looked around. "Where are you?" he asked. "Do you have gas?" Ash scrambled over rocks and peered around. "Let's talk this over. We need gas to get out of here."

Monte said nothing, Ash was closer than he liked.

After a moment Ash gave up and walked back to the jeep. It was still cool, but clambering over rocks had him sweating profusely. He got out of his coat and mopped his face.

"Better save that energy," Monte called out.

"Go to the devil!" Ash yelled. He scanned the rocks but had not yet figured out where Jackson was.

"We can go back to the spring where we left the jeep," Paula suggested in a low voice.

"You won't like the water. What do

you think I did with the gasoline?" Monte lied. They both spun around.

"Damn you! Who are you, and what's this all about?" Ash squinted at the area where Monte lay, he was looking right at him but couldn't make him out in the clutter of rocks and brush. They *must* know he knew who they were; what he was doing was fun but it was also serious business and rapidly growing tiresome.

Monte Jackson decided to stop fooling around and get down to business—he stood up.

"Write out a confession and we'll talk about water. I've got a canteen, and I know where you can get gas and fix your tank."

"So it is you? Well, you don't understand. You don't understand what you saw. We can explain. Just come down . . . come down here."

"I think I understand pretty well, Ash." The man jerked a bit when Monte used his name. "I think Mrs. Burgess there killed her husband for his life insurance and then the two of you went out looking for someone to take the blame . . . preferably a dead someone."

"You're crazy!" Ash shouted.

"Am I? I think murder is a crazy thing, myself. I also think a man's crazy to let a woman suck him into a mess like this."

He let that soak in for a moment. "You're an accessory, Ash, but, of course, they might believe you were in on it."

"I've an alibi!" Ash shouted, but his voice lacked confidence. "Come down and talk. There's money in this. We've got money right here. We can do business."

"Toss your pistol up here and I'll come."

Ash swore. Neither of them had believed he knew of the pistol. "Like hell!" Ash yelled.

"All right by me, but don't get any ideas. I've got a rifle."

Waiting would just make it hotter, and

after a while this seemed to dawn on them, yet the sun was blazing hot before they finally started. It was what he had hoped: to delay them until the sun was high.

"It's twenty miles to Keeler. Or you can strike south for the Death Valley highway, but you might get lost, too."

"Shut up!" Ash roared. "If I could get my hands on you, I'd . . . !"

"Get the beating of your life," Jackson said cheerfully. "Why, you're soft as butter, while I've drilled thousands of holes in hard rock by hand! You two think it over. A confession for water; you don't think it's a good deal now . . . but you will." He backed into cover then turned and walked off, climbing the ridge until he was a safe distance away and out of sight.

They seemed to be talking it over then; after about half an hour, they again started walking south, down the road. The man glanced around occasionally, worried, no doubt, that they both might get a bullet in the back. Well, let him worry.

Monte followed and did not try to hide his progress. Ash caught sight of him, paralleling their track about one hundred yards west and pointed him out to Paula. They didn't like it, but there was little they could do.

The sun was hot and Monte had long since folded his jacket into the haversack. Neither of them had a hat and he did, and unlike Ash, Monte kept his shirt sleeves rolled down. He picked up a piece of float and examined it. They were walking steadily, but Paula lagged a little, and he had an idea that Paula wanted to bargain on her own. Obviously, she wanted to talk.

Ash slowed. "Come on, honey! If we're going to get anywhere we've got to keep moving!"

"You go ahead. I'll be right behind. I can't walk fast in these shoes."

Ash walked on, Paula glanced around and Monte let his head show over the ridge. She stopped at once. "I want to talk to you," she invited. "Come on down!"

Selecting his spot, he sat down, making her come to him. When she was twenty yards away, he stopped her. "Close enough!" he said. "What do you want?"

Paula obviously wanted to come closer. She was accustomed to getting what she wanted from men, although after a night in a jeep she was considerably less attractive than he remembered her. "Why don't you forget this and come in with me?" she invited. "You've got a rifle, and we don't need him. There's a lot of money."

"What about that rap in L.A.?"

"We could say it was Ash. Come on, my husband was insured for seventy thousand dollars, and the house besides! Think what we could do with that!"

"Just think!" he said sarcastically. "Seventy thousand dollars, and us on the run for the rest of our lives. Funny, it doesn't sound like enough to me."

She stared at him, trying to figure him out. At that moment Ash showed over the last rise. When he saw them together he shouted and started to run toward them.

Jackson leaned his elbows on his knees and calculated the distance. The fool! Didn't he know he shouldn't run that hard in this heat? He watched him come. The effective range of a pistol is not great, but the actual range is greater than supposed. He would take no chances. He lifted the rifle. Ash slowed, then stopped, panting hoarsely. "No you don't!" he shouted. "You don't cross me up!"

Paula stared at him. "Quick!" she said eagerly. "Shoot him!"

"I'm sorry. I'm just not much interested

in money. And, it's really not that much money."

"It's enough!" she protested. ". . . and you could have me." She stepped forward, as if offering herself to him.

He grinned at her. "You should see yourself!" Her makeup was streaked and her hair mussed and dulled by dust. She'd been attractive back in the bar in Riverside, but here . . .

"I'd rather just take the money," he said.

She screamed, her face contorted, hurling epithets at him. Ash had come closer and now he brought up the pistol, so Monte stood, and with four sprinting steps was in the brush and rocks beyond the arroyo.

From his concealment he could hear their angry voices, and then Ash showed on the crest, the muzzle of his pistol a questing eye. His face was haggard and strained, his shirt soaked with sweat. He wouldn't sweat much longer.

Monte took a pull at the canteen and

rested in the shade of a clump of brush. Walking was okay but the running did not do his head any good. When he looked again they had started on and made almost half a mile. Paula Burgess looked beaten.

After a while he moved to follow, staying in the shade from the nearby ridge. When he again saw them they had stopped and were seated near some saltbush. They had reached the fork of the old desert trail.

From this point it branched south and then west to Keeler and north across the vast waste of the Saline Valley, waterless and empty. Paula had her shoes off and so did Ash. Obviously, they'd had enough although they'd come just five miles from the jeep. From where he crouched in the shadow of a rock he could see their faces were beginning to blister, and their lips looked puffed and cracked.

"How about it?" he called. "Want to

write out a confession, and sign it? I've got water, you know."

Neither made a reply, nor did they speak to each other.

He'd heard that it was typical of criminals that they are optimistic and always see themselves as successful. This seemed to have left these two with few resources when faced with failure.

"It's only three. Even once the sun goes down the heat will hang on because it takes time for the rocks to cool off. By six it should be better. If you're alive then."

"Give us a break!" Ash pleaded.

"You're not far from water. A couple of hundred feet straight down."

"Listen!" Ash got up. "I'd nothing to do with this! She roped me in on it, and I had no idea she was going to kill anybody!"

His voice was hoarse and it hurt him to speak. "That's tough," Monte agreed, "toss your gun over here and we'll discuss it."

"Nothing doing!"

"Forget it then. I won't even talk until I have that pistol."

Heat waves danced in the distance and a dust devil picked a swirl of dust from the valley floor and skipped weirdly across the desert until it died far away in the heat-curtained distance. Ash had moved nearer, and now Paula was hobbling toward him.

"Throw me the gun! Otherwise I'm going back to my claim!"

Ash hesitated, standing there with one hand in his pocket, his face drawn and haggard.

"You fool!" Paula screamed at him. "Give me that!" She grabbed the hand emerging from the pocket and before he could move to prevent her she pointed it at Monte.

He flattened out and the gun barked viciously. Sand stung his face and in a panic he rolled over into the low place behind him and, grabbing his rifle, broke into a run, dodging into the brush even as she topped the rise where he had been lying.

Ash shouted at her, but Paula was beyond reason, firing wildly. Monte hit shelter behind a boulder, then heard Paula scream once more, the gun sounded again and he looked back. They were standing on the rise, struggling furiously, with Paula clawing at his face. But then Ash was backing away, and he had the gun.

"Four shots," Monte warned himself. "There's more to come."

"Come on back! You can have the gun if you'll give us water!"

Monte was beyond easy pistol range. He got to his feet and lifted the rifle. "Fire another shot, and I leave you for the buzzards!"

He walked toward them, watching Ash. "Give me the gun and I'll tell you where there's water."

Ash hesitated no longer, but tossed the gun toward Monte. Jackson picked it up by the trigger guard, carefully wrapped it in his handkerchief and dropped it into the haversack.

Their faces were fiery red and there were ugly streaks on the man's cheek where it had been raked by Paula's fingernails. She stared at Monte, her eyes sullen with hatred. She was no longer pretty, for the desert sun and the bitterness of her hatred had etched lines into her face.

"There's water in the radiator of your jeep," he told them.

"Huh?" Hope flared, then died in the man's eyes. "Aw, hell, man, give us a break!"

"Like she gave her husband? Like you planned to give me? Many a man's been damned glad to get water out of a radiator and stay alive. It's only five miles from here."

He watched them, studying their faces. "Or, you can write out complete confessions, one for each of you, and then I'll see that you both drink."

Their faces were sullen. "You know," he added, "you're not really in a bad way yet. Soon it'll start getting complicated. You're losing salt, without it your bodies won't be able to process water even if I give you some . . . you could die of dehydration in a swimming pool." He took a salt pill out of his pocket and popped it into his mouth. "Soon water really won't be the problem."

They looked at each other in something approaching horror. He could see that they could just barely imagine what another two days would be like.

"That's not human!" Paula protested. "You can't do a thing like that to a woman!"

"Look who's talking! You started this!" He shook his head. "I don't care what happens to you. When a woman starts killing she is entitled to no special treatment."

He sat down on a rock, but it was much too hot and he got up immediately. Neither of them were sweating now. Their skins looked parched and dry. "Ash could probably get off with a few years. You'll have as much of a lawyer as you can buy, and who knows what a good lawyer can do. Out here it's a different thing . . . there's going to be no appeal when the sun comes up tomorrow."

Without warning, Ash leaped at him, swinging, and instantly, Paula darted forward, her eyes maniacal.

Monte sprang back and, swinging the rifle, clipped Ash alongside the head with the barrel. He turned, and sank the butt into Paula's stomach. They both went down, though Monte had pulled the blows. Ash wasn't even bleeding.

"Don't be foolish," he said. "Exertion will only make the end come quicker. You've both stopped sweating, that's usually a bad sign."

Ash cursed, glaring up at him from the ground.

Monte Jackson walked away and when thirty yards off, lifted the canteen and took a long pull, then sloshed the water audibly. They stared at him, their hatred displaced only by thirst. Knowing the desert, he knew neither of these people were as badly off as they believed, but by noon tomorrow . . .

"You think it over." He took a pad and pencil from his pocket, the pencil strapped to the pad with a rubber band. "When you're ready, start writing." He laid it on the ground.

Then he turned and walked into the desert toward a small corner of shade. His life, his freedom, everything depended on success, and if he failed now it would leave him in an even worse position with the law.

The hour dragged slowly by, then another half hour. They were no longer at the fork when he walked back, but their tracks were plain. They were returning to the jeep.

He turned off toward Dodd's Spring, drank, then refilled the canteen. They had taken the pad and pencil with them. He walked slowly after them; when he caught up, they were still a mile from the jeep, and both were seated. Ash, behind a clump of brush, was writing on the pad, squinting his eyes against the sun's glare on the paper.

The sheriff came at noon on the following day, driving up to Dodd's Spring in a jeep with Ragan on the seat beside him, and Slim Garner in the rear to show the way. Behind them was a weapons carrier with three more deputies. Monte Jackson walked down from the rocks to meet them.

"How are you, Jackson?" He had talked several times with the sheriff in Baker and elsewhere. "Ragan tells me you've had some trouble."

"Did Slim tell you what I told him?"

"He sure did. You know where they are?"

"Up the road a few miles. Let's go." He got into the jeep beside Garner. While they rode he handed the two confessions to Ragan. "That about covers it. Right now there's a chance they will both talk. Ash figures he will get off because he didn't actually kill anybody."

"We got a few facts," Ragan admitted. "Somebody planned to burn the house, all right. We found the oil-soaked rags and some spilled kerosene on the counter in the kitchen. Lucky for all of us the place didn't burn completely. Then we found out about Ash Clark, he's the guy down there, right? He promised his land-lady payment in a few days, said he was coming into money. It's definitely a case with a few loose ends."

Monte took the pistol from the haversack, and Ragan accepted it as the trucks rolled to a stop. Paula Burgess was haggard and the blazing desert sun had burned her fiercely. Ragan cuffed them and put them in with the deputies. Then they all turned and headed for town. Monte Jackson relaxed, looking back as the long desert road spun out behind the jeep. Long shadows stretched across the landscape, and dust devils danced like ghosts on the wide, sandy flats. A mirage glowed in the distance, looking for all the world like a cool and placid lake.

The desert, he thought, can be a friendly place . . . if only one showed it the proper respect.

WALTZ HIM AROUND AGAIN, SHADOW

Deke Murphy, wrangler for the Stockman's Rodeo in Bluff Springs, drew back against the corral, his keen gray eyes on the girl who was passing with Bill Bly, the rodeo star. In the three days he had been in town, Deke had seen the girl several times—and had fallen completely in love with her. As for Bly, Deke would not have liked him even if he had not been with Carol Bell.

The boots with their rundown heels, faded Levi's and his patched wool shirt made Murphy a distinct contrast to the immaculate gray of Bly's rodeo costume, but the contrast did not end there.

Bill Bly was a splendidly built man, two hundred and ten pounds of muscle, and easily over six feet. He was cock of the walk, looked it, acted it, and wanted it known. Bill Bly was the hero of the rodeo world and Deke Murphy was an unknown, a hard-faced youngster who had dropped off a freight train and rustled a job handling stock for the rodeo.

Bly and the girl halted by the corral and peered through the horizontal bars to watch the milling horses. "I'd like to ride that Highbinder horse," Bly told the girl. "He's the worst horse in this show an' a man could make a good ride up on him. The judges always watch the men who come out on bad horses. The Highbinder's never been rode."

He glanced tolerantly at Deke, who leaned against the corral, eyes for nothing and nobody but Carol Bell. "That Highbinder's plenty bad, ain't he, boy?"

Deke Murphy bristled. He disliked being called "boy." He was all of twenty-two, and they had been rough years, even by the standards of the West. "Not really," he said.

A shadow of dislike appeared in Bly's eyes. He was used to being yessed by the wranglers. "I suppose you could ride him?" he suggested sarcastically.

"I reckon," Deke said calmly. "Anyway, he's easy compared to that Shadow horse." He nodded toward the lean, narrow-headed grulla that idled alone near the far wall of the corral. "Shadow will pitch circles around him!"

Bly looked for the first time at the sleepy, mouse-colored horse. "Him? He couldn't buck four sour apples!" Bly glanced again at Murphy. "If you think you can ride the Highbinder," he said, with amusement, "you should be in the show! You'd be better than half the riders we've got! Maybe better than all of them!"

"Maybe," Deke said shortly, starting to

turn away. But Bly's voice stopped him, and he turned back.

"Just for fun," Bly said, "an' since you're such a good rider, I'll bet you twenty bucks you can't stay up ten seconds on Sonora, there."

Sonora, a mean-eyed buckskin with a splash of white on one hip, stared thoughtfully at them. Deke glanced at him.

"I can ride him," he said.

"Then put up your money! Talk is cheap!" Bly taunted.

Deke flushed. "I can ride him!" he said stubbornly, but he glanced left and right, looking for an escape.

"Come on!" Bly insisted, his eyes sneering at Deke under the guise of affability. "You said you could ride him! Let's see you do it! Put up your money!"

Several people had gathered around, and among them was a man of sixty-odd years, a white-haired man with keen blue eyes and a worn Stetson.

"Don't insist, Bill!" Carol said gently. "Maybe he doesn't feel like riding!"

"All right, honey." Bly looked back at Murphy. "Don't let me hear any more of that big talk! You got to put up or shut up," he said sharply.

Slowly the crowd drifted away and Deke Murphy turned miserably toward the corral, leaning against it, his head down. He had been made to look like a four-flusher. Anyway you take it, she would think he was a piker, a loud mouth. But how could he admit he didn't have twenty dollars? Or ten, or even five? How could he admit in front of Carol that he was broke?

She didn't know him, and she probably never would. She would not care, but he did. He cared desperately. From the first moment he had seen her, he knew she was the girl for him, and yet the gulf that separated them was bottomless.

"You think that Shadow horse can buck?" The voice was friendly.

Murphy looked up. "You just bet he can buck!" he said sharply. "Highbinder won't come near him!"

"You seen him?" the man persisted. It was the oldish man with the blue eyes and white hair, his brown face seamed and wind worn.

"Me? Why, uh, not exactly." Deke's words stumbled and he hesitated. "A friend of mine told me about him."

"I see." The old man nodded. "I'm Tim Carson. Been around long?"

"Just pulled in," Deke admitted, "I don't know nobody here. Saw this rodeo, an' braced 'em for a job feedin' an' waterin' stock."

"Got any money?"

Deke's head came up sharply, his eyes cold and bitter. "That just ain't none of your business!" he said.

Carson shrugged. "If you had money you wouldn't get so het up about it," he said. "Figured you might need a few bucks for grub an' such."

Murphy studied him suspiciously.

"What do I have to do?" he demanded. "I won't do nothing crooked an' I won't take money for nothin'."

"I figured on a loan, but if you want to earn it—" Carson waved a hand at the buckskin. "Throw a saddle on that horse an' I'll pay off if you ride him."

"How much?" Deke demanded.

"Oh, say twenty bucks!" Carson suggested.

"What you want to see me ride him for?" Deke asked cautiously.

"See if I'm right or not," Carson said. "I figure I know folks. I figure the only reason you wouldn't get up on that horse was because you didn't have the money to bet an' wouldn't admit it in front of that girl."

"Old man," Deke said, "you figure too darn close. Now put up your money."

"It's in my pocket," Carson said. "You get a saddle an' we'll ride this horse."

Without another word Deke went off

to get a saddle, and as he walked away Carol Bell came from between the buildings, slapping her boots with a quirt. "Uncle Tim," she demanded, "what are you up to now? Why do you want that boy to ride that horse?"

Deke Murphy came back trailing a saddle which he grasped by the horn, and with a bridle over his shoulder. With the help of Carson he saddled and bridled the buckskin. The arena was empty at this early hour and Deke climbed the bars of the chute to mount the horse. Carol had drawn back to one side, and he had not seen her. He dropped into the saddle and Carson turned the horse loose.

The buckskin made a run for the center of the arena, skidded to halt with his head down, and when his rider stayed in the saddle, scratching with both heels, the buckskin swapped ends three times as fast as he could move and then buck-jumped all over the arena, ending his spurt and the ten seconds by sunfishing wildly for three full seconds. Carson yelled, and Deke unloaded hurriedly.

Together they caught up the buckskin and led him back to the corral. "They'll raise Old Nick when they find out I rode this horse!" Deke said worriedly.

"Forget it. I know them." He dug into his pocket—"An' here's your twenty bucks, son. Good luck!"

"Thanks," Deke said, gripping the twenty and staring at it with unbelieving eyes. "Man, that's the fastest money I ever made!"

Carson studied him. "You ride mighty well, son. Ever do any ridin' in a rodeo?"

Deke looked up, hesitated, then shook his head. "Not exactly," he replied. "I'd better beat it. I've got a lot of work to do an' I want to go up to town for a little bit!"

Tim Carson watched him go, glanced toward the place where his niece had been watching, and seeing she was gone, he turned toward the office with purposeful strides. "It's him!" he said grimly. "I'd bet money it's the same kid!"

Deke Murphy walked down the town's dusty, banner-hung street and turned into a general store. "I want to buy a new pair of Levi's," he said, "an' a shirt, a good shirt!"

A half an hour later, with the new clothes on and a good meal under his belt, he walked back to the corrals. It would soon be time for the parade down the main street that would end at the rodeo grounds, and then the Grand Entry Parade that would open the show. He would have much to do.

In his pocket were three dollars and some change, but he felt better. Still a far cry from the glamorous clothes of the rodeo stars, his were at least neat, and he looked much better than in the shabby clothes he had been wearing, too redolent of the stable, and slept in too many times.

There was a job to do here, and he had to get on with it. He shook his head over his dislike of Bill Bly. It would never do to have trouble with him. All he knew was horses and cattle, and if he made an enemy of Bly he would be blackballed around every rodeo in the country. And he wanted very much to stick close to rodeos. The man he was looking for was somewhere around them, and if he looked long enough, somehow he would find him. Wherever the man was, he still wore the brand Deke Murphy had given him.

Tim Carson watched him return to his job in the new clothes and studied him through careful eyes. The build was similar. The kid was lean and rugged, muscular, but not big. He carried himself well and moved well. It could be the same one.

Bill Bly watched his horse being saddled for him and then turned to greet Carol as she walked up. "Hello, Bill." She smiled up at him. "Say, it's lucky that kid didn't take you up on your bet this morning. Uncle Tim offered him twenty dollars to ride the buckskin, and the kid rode him—scratched him high, wide, and handsome!"

Bly's brows tightened a little. "He did? Well, good for him!" His words were affable, but there was none of that in his mood. Deke had irritated him, and he did not like being irritated. Moreover, he had decided that Deke was a loudmouth and he disliked being proved wrong.

Another idea struck him. "Why did your uncle do that?"

"Oh, there's no accounting for Uncle Tim! He's liable to do anything! But it isn't that this time: he's interested in this fellow, I can see it. He was watching him like a cat all the time."

"I wonder why?" Bly remarked absently. He was thinking of how he would look in the parade with this girl beside him. Old Curly Bell's only child—not a bad idea, marrying her.

"I don't know," Carol said, "but Uncle Tim's funny. He used to be a United States marshal, you know. Over in Nevada."

Bly turned abruptly. "In Nevada, you say?" He caught himself. "You'd never suspect it. He seems so quiet."

"I know, but he's that way. He's still angry, and has been for the past three years over that gold shipment robbery."

"Oh, yes! I recall something about it, I think. The bandits held up a train and got away with two hundred thousand dollars in freshly minted gold, wasn't that it?"

"I guess so. Uncle Tim believes that gold is still intact and has never been used, that it is cached somewhere."

"But he's not even an officer anymore, is he?"

"No, but that doesn't matter to Uncle Tim. In fact, I've heard him say more than once that he believed the thieves would come back, that the gold was hidden someplace not too far from here, in the mountains."

"You think that's why he's interested in this Murphy kid? One of the bandits was supposed to be no more than a boy. He was the one who killed the messenger."

"Oh, no!" The protest was sharp, dismayed. For some reason the idea frightened and disturbed Carol. It had not occurred to her before that such might be the reason for her uncle's interest in Deke Murphy.

Carol Bell would not have admitted her interest in Deke Murphy even to herself. In fact, she was scarcely aware of that interest, yet she remembered what he had practically told her uncle, that Deke had not wanted to be shown up as being broke in front of her.

She was a thoroughly aware young lady, and had seen his eyes follow her from place to place, and his interest pleased her. Moreover, he *could* ride. She had seen him ride, and she was enough of a rider herself to know that he would compare favorably with many of the contest hands.

In the office, after calling his wire through to the telegraph office, Tim Carson turned to Tack Hobson. "Hobby," he said, "you know that Shadow horse? How many shows has he been in and where were they?"

"Funny you should ask that," Hobson remarked, "but he's never been ridden by anybody, an' he's shown in just four rodeos . . . all of them in prisons."

"I see. Was the Highbinder in any of these shows?"

"One of them. He was ridden once by a convict." Hobson stoked his pipe. "Reason I said it was funny you should ask is that you're the second man who asked that question. Bill Bly was in here, just a few minutes ago. He wanted to know the same thing."

Deke Murphy had no idea just how he was to find his man, or exactly what he would do when he found him. From the moment he had been released from prison that had been his one idea. He had been framed and framed badly, and had done two years for a crime in which he had no part.

It had been a dark night when he had ridden up from his last camp near Singing Mountain, a tough and lonely kid, eager only to escape from his home in the Robber's Roost country and to find an honest job. Riding since he could first remember, he had lived a lonely life back in the breaks with his mother and his step-father.

His stepfather had been a kindly man around home, and despite the fact that he was a rustler, had been a good father and a good husband, yet Deke's mother had reared him to be an honest man, and had made him promise that when he was old enough he would leave the Roost behind and start out on his own. His mother had died of pneumonia, alone and unattended except by himself, and his stepfather had been killed in a gunfight shortly after. Deke, true to his promise, had left the Roost behind.

He rode for a ranch in Utah, then one in Nevada, and started down the country looking to get himself as far from the Roost as possible. Leaving Singing Mountain, broke and without food, he had come upon an outlaw camp on the site of Sand Springs.

Three men had loafed by the fire. Deke knew all three, and about only one of them could he say anything good. Frank Wales had been a friend of his father's, an outlaw, but a man of some decency. Jerry Haskell and Cass Kubela he knew mostly by reputation but their reputation wasn't anything his mother would have approved of.

"Hey," Kubela had said, sitting up, "how about the kid? When we take the next shipment he could be the fifth man."

Wales glanced at him. "The kid's no outlaw," he said. "Leave him out of this!"

Jerry Haskell was a lean, dry whip of a man with a saturnine expression in his black eyes. He had killed two men that Deke knew about. "He's in now," he said, "he knows us an' he's seen us. Whether he likes it or not, he's in."

"I'm in nothing!" Deke had said hotly. "I'm ridin' through. Figured I might get me a bait of grub, then ride on. I ain't seen nothin', don't know nothin'!"

At Wales' invitation, he ate, eager only

to finish and get away. That the three were waiting for their leader to get back, he knew. That they had just committed a robbery and were planning the holdup of a shipment from the mines, he soon learned. He knew Wales was his only friend here, but the older man would not dare go against the two seasoned outlaws. Cass Kubela had killed more than one man. A short, tough fellow with narrow eyes and big hands, he was even more dangerous than Haskell. Of the three here, Wales was without doubt the weakest link.

When he had eaten he rose to go, but Kubela motioned to him to sit down. "Stick around, kid," he advised, and the suggestion had been an order. Deke Murphy, his heart pounding, had sat down. The shotgun lying across Kubela's knees added emphasis to the command.

Later, when he had dozed off, he opened his eyes enough to know the fourth man had returned. He overheard a few words. "His old man was a weak sister," someone was saying, "the kid's ma preached to him. I say we can't trust him."

Wales' protest was overruled, but then the fourth man spoke. "Keep him for now, we can use him. Get some sleep and we'll move out early. . . . They may still be on my trail."

Although he waited and listened, Deke heard no more, and somewhere along the trail of his waiting, he fell asleep again. He awakened to a confusion of shots, and for one startled instant, he stared around wildly, then grabbed his boots and tugging them on, made a break for his horse.

Another man, a big man, came charging up, and he too grabbed at Deke's horse. "That's my horse!" Deke protested.

The man turned half around, but in the darkness Deke Murphy could not see his face. "Shut up, you fool!" he snapped, and he slashed viciously at Deke with the barrel of his gun.

It caught the boy a glancing blow across the skull and lights exploded in his brain. As he started to go down, he grabbed out and got a hand in the edge of the big man's pocket. He jerked and the pocket ripped, and the man toppled back to the ground. He sprang up and aimed a vicious kick at the boy's head, but Deke lunged to his feet and struck out hard. The blow landed, and Deke followed it in. His unknown antagonist smashed up with his right, and then the gun bellowed, fired by their struggles. With a curse of panic the man flung him off and sprang into the saddle. There was a rattle of hoofs and he was gone!

An instant later a half-dozen men charged down on Deke. He was surrounded, searched, and taken away. Later, tried and convicted, he was sentenced to five years in the penitentiary for a holdup that had been committed the previous day. His stepfather's record was known. He admitted his acquaintance with all the robbers but one, and his denials that he had any part in the holdup were laughed out of consideration.

The man he sought was the leader of the band, the man who had stolen his horse and left him to be captured and sentenced to prison. His sole clue was a comment made by Kubela on that memorable night when half awake he heard them talking. Kubela had said, "The boss can ride, alright! He's a top contest hand!" And it was that boss who had left him for the law, and while the posse was making him a prisoner, the actual outlaws escaped.

Frank Wales, the only man who could have testified to his actual connection with the robbers, was now dead. He had escaped only to be killed near the ghost town of Hamilton two years before, resisting arrest.

• • •

Tim Carson sauntered down to the chutes and stopped near chute three where Deke Murphy was working. "You should be riding in this show, kid. There's some good prizes!"

"You know I'm broke," Deke said sullenly. "How could I enter?"

"Suppose I paid your entry fees?" Carson persisted. "Would you ride?"

"You're darn tootin' I would!" Deke said. His eyes followed the leaders of the Grand Parade, looking enviously at Bill Bly riding beside Carol Bell. The girl's eyes happened to turn his way, and she smiled. Deke felt his heart leap. "You loan me that money, mister! I'll pay you back out of my winnin's!"

Carson watched the parade thoughtfully, and for a minute or two he did not speak. Then he said, "You're entered, Murphy. I already paid your fees. You're entered in every event, take what you want of them!"

Deke stared, his eyes incredulous. "You mean, you—" He hesitated, uncertain what to say.

"I like to see a kid get his chance," Carson said, "an' that in particular when he's had bad breaks. You get on out there, let's see you bust 'em wide open!"

An hour later, hurrying up to Tim Carson's place by the chute, Carol caught his arm. "Uncle Tim! Did you enter that boy in the rodeo? Did you?"

Carson smiled gravely. "I sure did, honey, an' if you want to gamble I'll bet you he puts Bly in the shade!"

Carol said nothing, her eyes following the young rider who was saddling the roping horse Carson had provided for him. "Uncle Tim, do you think he is one of those men who robbed that two hundred thousand dollars?"

Carson took the pipe from his mouth. "Now where'd you get that idea? An' whoever told you it was two hundred thousand?"

"Bill did, but I got the idea from you. You've never let that old crime rest. I know it still bothers you."

"It does at that." Carson returned his pipe to his teeth. "Carol, I hate crooks. I also hate like poison anyone who'll let an innocent man do his time. You asked me if I thought Deke was one of them, an' I'll tell you: I *know* he wasn't. But he's been in prison for it, an' I've a hunch he's huntin' the man who led that holdup—a man we know as Jud Kynell, one of the old bunch that hung out at the Roost."

"He was in prison?" Carol watched the young rider, her eyes serious. "Do you suppose—I mean, do you think he's honest now? I—I know some men become thieves or worse while in jail."

"Honey, I think the boy's honest. He wouldn't take money from me without working for it."

Deke walked toward them, leading his

horse. He grinned shyly at the girl. On impulse, Carol removed her handkerchief and handed it to him, then took it back and knotted it about his neck herself.

"You need something that shows you're riding for us now," she said. "Good luck." For a breathtaking instant they were very close, and as she pulled the knot into place, she looked up at him. His face was pale and he looked almost frightened.

"Ma'am," he said sincerely, "you watch me! I'll kick the frost out of anything they've got—for you!"

Before the contest was more than a few minutes old the entire arena had awakened to the fact that out there on the tanbark a fierce duel was beginning, a duel between tall, powerful Bill Bly, and the unknown newcomer.

"Ladies and gents! Billy Bly, star of rodeo and stock corral, makes his tie in eleven and six-tenths seconds!" Hobson, the announcer, drew a breath and then continued to bellow into the small end of his speaking trumpet. "That's the fastest time so far today, and ties the record for this here arena!"

He turned and waved a hand. "Now out of the chutes—Deke Murph!"

Carson's horse was a sorrel streak, and Deke's rope shot out like a thrown lance, the loop opening just as the calf dodged, and dropped over its head! Murphy stepped down as his horse put on the brakes, dropped to one knee alongside the calf, and made his tie. As he sprang back, dust rising from the bound calf, a gasp went over the arena.

Hobson's voice boomed out. "Well, folks! Now there's a *record*! Deke Murphy at eleven and four-tenths seconds, to win the first go-around!"

Amid cheers, Murphy swung into the saddle and cantered across to where Carol stood waiting with her uncle Tim and Bly. Bly looked up, the same cold expression in his eyes, his lips forcing a smile. "Nice going," he commented, but his voice was flat.

"Oh, Deke! You were *wonderful!*" Carol exclaimed.

Bly won the steer wrestling, with Deke a close second, and Red Roller, a big cowhand from Cheyenne, a tight third. In the Brahma riding, Deke came out on No. 66, an ugly mass of bull meat weighing all of two thousand pounds and a fighter as well as a rodeo veteran.

He knew what he was out there for and he went at it with a will, buck-jumping and twisting his tail. Deke was hanging on for dear life and the bull was out to ditch him or die. Somehow, Deke stayed up until the whistle blew.

He threw a leg over the bull's back, hit the ground, and the bull swapped ends and came for him. The clowns rushed in with flapping cloaks and slapping hats to draw the animal's attention. It sprang this way and that, trying desperately to get at his enemies, not so much in torment as in sheer enjoyment of battle and lust for conquest.

Deke limped back to the chute, grinning at Carol, his face dusty and a trickle of blood coming from his nose. "Rough!" he said, shaking his head.

"You made a good ride," Carson admitted. "Bly's drawn Highbinder for the bronc riding."

"Who did I get?" Deke demanded, looking up quickly. Then he grinned wryly. "As if I didn't know!"

"Shadow," Carson confessed, "you'll be up on Shadow!"

"Highbinder's the worst horse," Bly said casually. "Whoever heard of Shadow?"

"I did." Murphy clipped the words. "I've seen him buck. Highbinder won't touch him."

"As if you knew," sneered Bly, his eyes cold.

"I do." Deke snapped the words. "I rode him!"

"What?" Bill Bly put an open hand to Deke's chest and pushed, backing him up. "Why, you little liar! You—"

Deke's balled fist smashed him in the mouth and the big man staggered. Then Bly straightened, his eyes utterly vicious. "Now you've done the wrong thing!" he said. "I'll beat your head in!"

Bly rushed, swinging. His right was a long arc that encountered nothing but air. Deke Murphy rose inside of Bly's arms and landed a series of short, wicked punches to the stomach and ribs. Bly clinched and hurled Deke back into the corral fence with sheer strength, then charged.

Again Deke, working coolly, went under the blow, and again he smashed away at Bly's ribs with those strength-sapping short punches. This time he ducked away before Bly could clinch, and when Bly swung a left, Deke caught it on his right forearm, and chopped down with a wicked punch to the big man's chin.

Bly blinked, he was bleeding from his split lips, and stared confusedly through the sweat and his hanging hair at the much shorter man.

"You want some more?" Deke asked calmly. "Or have you had enough?"

Deke looked him over coolly, then turned and walked away. As he drew near to Carol he paused. "Sorry," he said, "I didn't want trouble!"

Bly shook his head to clear it and stared after him. "Jailbird!" he sneered. "High-binder was never rode but once! In prison!"

Deke's face was white and still. He turned, and his voice was low but clear. "That's right," he said, "that was where I rode him!"

As he headed for the stable, staring grimly ahead, Deke passed close by two men whom he did not see. Jerry Haskell and Cass Kubela watched him go. "It's him, all right," Cass said. "The Boss was right. It's the kid!"

"He knows us," Haskell said.

Kubela's eyes were cold. He took the cigarette from his lips and dropped it into the dust. "Not for long!"

Carson stood by, watching Deke bathe his face and hands, smoking quietly. When Deke had dried himself he looked at Carson.

"Now you know, I was in prison."

"Knew it all the time. I even knew your stepfather."

"You what?"

"Sure. Knew your ma, too. He wasn't a bad man . . . just didn't stop rustling when it went out of style."

Tim Carson smoked thoughtfully. "Son, at the trial you said you knew the men who robbed that train, but you wasn't with them. You named Cass Kubela an' Jerry Haskell."

"Right." Deke waited, curiously.

"Now I've never seen those hombres. Until that job they always worked east of the mountains. Would you know them again?"

"I reckon I would."

"How about their boss? You said at the trial you didn't know him but that he was Jud Kynell. Folks thought you were coverin' up. Were you?"

"No. Robber's Roost covered miles, an' outlaws used to work back an' forth from the Hole in the Wall to the Roost an' clean down over the old horse-thief trail to the border. We heard about a lot of men we never saw. Jud Kynell was around when I was a kid. He's some ten years older than me, as I figure it."

"Know anything about him?"

"That's about all, except that he did

this; rodeoin' I mean. That and he wears my brand." Deke explained about what he had overheard, and his belief that the outlaw wore a deep scar on his chest. "There was an awful lot of blood for a scratch," he finished. "I figure it ripped pretty deep."

"That's an item." Carson was thoughtful. "Son, I got a tip that Kubela was headed this way, ridin' with another man."

"Haskell, most likely." Deke looked at Carson. "You better watch it. Those two are killers."

"I know." Carson got up. "Kid, can you sling that gun you're wearin'?"

Deke smiled. "Some . . . what have you got in mind?"

"I'm goin' to swear you in as a deputy. Everybody figures I'm no longer an officer . . . you see this?"

The older man held forth a wallet containing a badge and some papers, "Deputy U.S. Marshal. It's my theory those two were comin' here, an' comin' to meet their boss, get that gold an' hightail it out of the country. I trailed those boys to the vicinity of Forlorn Hope Spring in the foothills of the Opal Mountains, an' I'd bet that gold ain't cached more than a few miles from there."

Bill Bly's ride on Highbinder was something to see, for the big red horse was a fighter, and Bly, say what one would of the man, was a rider. They went out of the chute like a miniature explosion and the red horse leaped for the sun. He landed and swapping ends he let go with both hind feet, almost standing on his head.

Then he settled down to a wild, unrestrained and wholly murder-minded job of bucking. Eyes rolling, the beast went to work with a will, but when the whistle blew Bly was still on deck.

Bly walked back to the chute with the

crowd's roaring cheers around him. It had been a great ride, a wicked ride. As he passed a small group of men not far from the chute, he saw Jerry Haskell. The lean-faced man nodded toward the opposite end of the arena, and tapped his pistol butt.

Bly walked on to where Shadow, an evil-eyed grulla, was being saddled for Deke Murphy, who perched on the side of the chute. Deke dropped into the saddle as Bly glared up at him. "Nice ride!" Deke said. "Too bad Highbinder was feelin' sort of poorly!"

"Shut up, you fool!" Bly snapped.

Deke's head came up with a jerk and his mouth opened in astonishment. Those words!

"You ready?" Red Roller glared at him. "Better get your mind on your business, boy! This one's a fighter!"

"I'm ready!" Murphy was suddenly grim and cold. "Give 'im air!"

Shadow was a horse with a mission. He hated men, all men, but he reserved a special and bitterly vindictive brand of hate for those who tried to ride him. He came out of that chute like a rattlesnake with the DT's and went to sunfishing.

He jumped straight up, all four legs hanging and his back bowed like an angry cat. Hitting the ground he went straight up again as if lifted by a charge of powder.

Deke hung on as the horse twisted his whipcord body sharply to the left. Switching and humping, that bronc went to work to give the crowd a show and to beat his rider into submission. He bucked straightaway, seesawing wickedly as he jumped, and contorted his back and writhed his spine.

He headed north with a wicked forward jump, then sprang straight back and swapped ends three times. Deke felt air under him and for one frantic instant thought he was a goner, but then he slapped the saddle with the seat of his Levi's and the world around him was a crazy quilt of tossing color and blurred shadows where nothing seemed to exist but that writhing, twisting, fighting explosion beneath him.

Somewhere far off he heard a whistle blowing and suddenly the horsemen were tearing toward him.

But Shadow was not through. Shadow had his own ideas about quitting and this was not the time or the place. He swapped ends and headed for the stands on a dead run, with the horsemen swinging to follow.

At the wall of the stands, he swung broadside and hurled himself at the board. Deke, in a long leap, grabbed at the front rail of the stands and left the saddle with a bound, leaving the frustrated, screaming horse behind him to be gathered up by the riders.

Dazedly, he stared around at the cheering crowd, then he managed a grin. He pulled his hat from his head and lifted it, and then as his hand came down, his face went blank with astonishment. There was a bullet hole through the crown!

Instantly, he remembered.

Shut up, you fool!

Wheeling, he vaulted over the rail and dropped to the ground. His hand felt for his gun, and it was still with him. He started across the arena, walking fast. Bill Bly stood alone, staring at him. Behind Bly, back by the barns, Carson held a pistol on Haskell. Haskell slowly lowered a rifle to the ground. Deke stood there looking at Bly.

Suddenly, the noise of the crowd seemed gone, and he stood alone in the sun-washed stillness, his legs spread, staring at the man who faced him. Out of the tail of his eye he saw a man step slightly away from the crowd, partly under cover of the stands. It was Cass Kubela.

"I know you now," Deke said.

"You're crazy!"

"Open your shirt then, an' if you've no scar on the left side of your chest, I'll apologize."

"Go to the devil!" Bly said viciously.

Between them a cigarette lay in the dust, lifting a thin column of hazy smoke upward. A horse stomped in a chute, and somewhere a child cried in petulant irritation. And then out of the corner of his eye, Deke saw Kubela's gun coming up.

Kubela's gun came up, and Deke pivoted on the ball of his left foot and fired from hip level. He felt Kubela's bullet hit him, and he fired again. The outlaw took a staggering step forward and fell headlong, the gun dribbling from his fingers.

Bly, with a snarl of fury, had grabbed for his gun. As it swung up, Deke came around and fired!

Bly took it standing, a little puff of dust leaping from his gray shirt. Bly stepped forward, seemed to hesitate, then his knees wilted under him and he folded up like a punctured accordion.

Dazed, Deke turned, thumbing shells automatically into his gun. The crowd was pouring from the stands, moving desperately to get out of the way of any more shooting.

Deke's leg felt numb, and he turned and stared down at it. There was no blood or sign of injury, and then he saw the smashed silver ornament on his belt over his right hip where the bullet had struck and glanced off.

Tim Carson rushed up to him. "You hurt, boy? Did he get you?"

"No." Deke limped over to Jud Kynell's body. Bending over, he pulled back the shirt. There on the man's chest was a ragged white scar made by the muzzle blast of his gun on that night long ago when he and Deke had struggled over it. "Funny, I never figured Bly was my man," he said. "Not until I heard his voice just before I came out on Shadow."

"I knew," Carson said, "in fact we've been pretty sure for over a year, but just lacked the right dope on him. Then he talked to Carol today about the holdup, an' he mentioned it was two hundred thousand. That was kept secret, an' nobody ever knew but the outlaws an' the government. Just one man at the mines actually knew an' he kept his mouth shut. Tyin' that in with what else we knew, it had to be him."

Carol's hand was on his arm, and he looked down. "You know," he said, "wearin' your colors brought me luck, I think."

"Then why not keep wearing them?" she asked.

"Well, ma'am," he said, smiling, "that's not a bad idea . . . and it's probably safer to ride when there's no one shootin' at you!"

DOWN PAAGUMENE WAY

Steve Cowan leaned back against a packing case on the jetty at Paagumene Bay, New Caledonia, lazily watching the shipping. It was growing dark, and would soon be night.

Five ships were anchored in the harbor, all of them with cargoes for American troops. One, her freight discharged, was loading chrome from lighters.

The last rays of sunshine tipped the masts with transient gold. The freighter loading ore would sail tonight. In a few weeks she would be tying up in an American port.

Steve Cowan's eyes strayed to the amphibian, riding lightly on the darkening water. A little refitting and he could fly her home on furlough, his first since being assigned to Army Intelligence. She was a beautiful plane, resembling the Grumman "Widgeon" but built to certain unusual specifications, laid down by Army designers. Because of that she was much faster and more maneuverable than any ship of her type. Moreover, she was armed like a fighter, and had a small bomb bay, so far unused except for freight.

A few changes to accommodate more fuel instead of the load of bombs she was built to carry, and he could fly her home.

Four years ago he had come out to the Pacific, and they had been four years of unceasing activity. Years that culminated in the Japanese invasion of the East Indies, ending his express and mail-carrying business suddenly and dramatically. Since being commissioned, he had acted as a secret messenger and under-cover agent for the Allies.

It would be good to be back in the States again, to walk down the streets, to get away from the heat and humidity, eat a cheeseburger, and have a cold soda or beer.

A boat bumped alongside the jetty and two men clambered out.

"You just get that chrome to the right place at the right time. You get it there, or else."

Abruptly, Steve Cowan stiffened. He knew that voice! Instinctively, he shrank down further behind the packing case.

"You don't understand!" the second man protested. "This job is a cinch. It won't interfere with the chrome deal. We can pick up the classified sailing list from the butler in Isola Mayne's place. With those Jap credentials we got, nobody'd be the wiser. The Japs'll pay heavy to get it back. They got to have it for their subs!"

"Yeah?" the voice sneered. "You pull

something like that, *Meyer*," an odd inflection was put on the name, as if Meyer was being taunted, "Koyama will cut your heart out. Try it and see what happens."

Something in the tone of that ugly, domineering voice rang a bell of memory in Steve Cowan's brain.

Mataga!

Recognition brought a start of dismay. Not twenty feet away, on the edge of the jetty was a man sworn to kill Cowan on sight. And Cowan was unarmed.

Mataga was speaking again. "You do what you're told. All you have to worry about is getting this cargo of chrome to the Japs."

"Besi John" Mataga in New Caledonia! Steve Cowan's eyes narrowed. The renegade from the waters around Singapore was not one to stop at anything. Deadly, brutal, and efficient, he had been working with Jap and Nazi Fifth Columnists for several years. When Singapore fell he went to Saigon. When Java succumbed, he appeared in Batavia. Now he was here, in New Caledonia!

As their footsteps receded down the jetty, Steve Cowan got to his feet. If Besi John was here it meant something big was moving. Something infinitely more important than a shipload of chrome. If he was working with Koyama it meant even more, for the Japanese was a leader of the powerful and notoriously evil Black Dragon Society, which had many underground members in the South Seas. And "Meyer"? Could that be Captain Peter Meyer . . . ?

The eyes of M. Esteville were amused when Cowan met with him the next day. "But, m'sieu," he protested gently, "it cannot be! The vessel you speak of is the *Benton Harbor*, well known to us." He sighed gustily. "As you say, it is true her master is Peter Meyer, a native of

Holland, but he is highly respected here. Your story, if you'll forgive me, is utterly preposterous!"

"I know Mataga," Cowan persisted. "And I know what I heard."

Esteville shrugged. "Undoubtedly Mataga is a dangerous criminal. But here? I think not. It would be too dangerous. A fancied resemblance, no more."

"Bah!" Steve Cowan's voice was flat. "I know Mataga. Last night I heard him speaking. As to the other man, he may be your Captain Meyer, or he may not. I know Mataga is here and something's in the wind."

"We will investigate." Esteville stood up, plainly annoyed. "But you are mistaken. Nothing is wrong with that ship. As for your wild tale about the shipping lists, that is fantastic. Even if such information could be obtained, there are no spies in Paagumene."

Cowan's eyes hardened. The man's indifference annoyed him. "I've told you. Now do something, or I will!"

Esteville's eyes blazed. "Remember, m'sieu, that New Caledonia still has a government! We are capable of handling our own affairs. Any interference from you will bring a protest to American officials—a protest too strong to be ignored."

Cowan turned on his heel and walked out. He could scarcely blame Esteville for being doubtful. Cowan's connection with Army Intelligence was secret and, because of strict orders, Cowan did not dare tell him. After all, Captain Meyer, master of the *Benton Harbor,* had an excellent reputation and Esteville might feel justified in rejecting such a wild story without proof.

Thoughtfully Cowan paused under a tree and considered his next step. Summing up, how much did he actually know? That the *Benton Harbor* was the only ship in the roadstead being loaded with chrome, a vital war material, and that she would soon leave for the United States. Also that Besi John, a notorious criminal and Fifth Columnist, was here on shady business.

A shipping list had been mentioned, too, and enemy agents. One of whom was evidently working in conjunction with Japanese submarines, plying along the southern route to Australia. Esteville had said there were no spies and that such a list would be impossible to obtain. Yet Besi John had spoken of both agents and list in a matter-of-course manner. So they *did* exist. How could Cowan find out more about them?

Then he remembered Isola Mayne.

He had never seen her. Pictures, of course. Everyone had seen pictures of Isola Mayne. She was more than a beautiful woman, more than a great actress. She was a legend.

Three years before, she had abruptly retired and, going to Singapore, had settled down, apparently for life. Then came the Japanese invasion, and Isola, in her own plane, had flown to Palembang, and next to Soerabaja. When she arrived in Sydney she moved the war off the front pages. Then she was gone. She vanished into nothingness.

A few days the world wondered, but with the war, they soon forgot.

Yet Steve Cowan knew where she was. He knew, because he had flown supplies to her plantation on New Caledonia. He had not seen her, but knew she was living there in seclusion. And Isola Mayne's brother was Port Captain! Married to a French woman, he too had spent time in Singapore, before that La Rochelle, and then relocated to Paagumene. In these places he had held prominent maritime positions. The spy must be one of the servants of his household, one who had managed in some way to steal a copy of the sailing list.

Unconsciously, Cowan had wandered back to the jetty. He stopped, staring at the dark blobs—freighters on Paagumene Bay. Much more was at stake out at the Oland Point home of Isola Mayne and her brother than appeared on the surface. A sailing list, in the hands of the Japanese submarine commanders, might disrupt the whole military line of supplies with the Far East. Whichever enemy got it— either the Japanese or Besi John Mataga— did not matter much with Cowan. Either way it would be disastrous.

Mataga was on the island, and somewhere nearby was Koyama. Mataga's apparent lack of interest in the list had not fooled Cowan. He knew the man too well. Besi John, *besi* being Malay for "iron," would make his own attempt in his own way, and Mataga would strike with utter ruthlessness.

Cowan took his cigarette from his mouth and snapped it into the bay. He could do nothing here. Oland Point was where the answer would be.

He dropped into the rubber boat and paddled out to the amphibian.

Opening the door of the cabin, he stepped in. A light flashed suddenly in his eyes and a fist smashed out of the darkness and knocked him to his knees. Someone struck him a vicious blow on the head, then another.

Through a fog of pain he struggled to hold himself erect, he heard Mataga's harsh voice.

"Lash. the beggar!" Besi John growled. "We got a date at Oland Point."

Cowan struggled, trying to shout. Then something crashed upon his skull and he fell forward into a foam of pain that ate into and through him.

• • •

It was almost day when he opened his eyes again. The plane was still in the air. Struggling to master his nausea, he tried to reason things out. Still in the air?

He struggled to rise, but an arrow of torment from his head made him fall back, helpless. But not before he had discovered that he was tied hand and foot.

His brow furrowed, he tried to grope his way back along the trail of semiconsciousness. Something had happened—

Memory of it was veiled in the mists, in the half-lights of awareness after he had been struck down. How long, he could not recall, yet something had happened. There was a dim recollection of lapping water, a strange dream of firelight dancing upon a dark hull, a mutter of motors, aircraft engines, and the murmur of voices.

He remembered, vaguely, through darkness and clouds, a round hump, like that on a camel's back.

Somehow, that dark hump stood out in his mind, forcing itself always into the foreground. He had a feeling of having seen it before.

Finally he opened his eyes, and knew that he had passed out again. The plane was resting on the water. He could hear waves lapping against the hull.

He rolled over, and tipping his head back, Cowan looked around the cabin of the plane. Sitting in the hatchway, with his legs dangling toward the water was a huge and heavily tattooed Malay. Seeing that he was, for the moment, unobserved, the pilot tried to move his hands. They were bound beneath him and the tightness of the ropes was cutting into his wrists but more painful than that was a seam in the folded metal of the aircraft . . . a seam that just might have a sharp enough edge to free him!

Moving with the slight swell of the water under the craft, Steve Cowan shifted until the ropes lay across the seam, and then, very slowly, he began to saw up and down. How long he worked he did not know but the progress was horribly slow. He felt strands of the rope part, but when he twisted his wrists they seemed just as tightly held. Dispirited, he glanced up and noticed the native in the door watching him with a knowing sneer on his face . . . and the Malay watchman was a man he knew!

Yosha was a tough from the oil fields in Balikpappan, a man noted for his viciousness and dishonesty. With a war on it was not surprising that he and Besi John had washed up on the same shore.

"So, y'get away, eh?" Yosha stood and started aft, his blocky body filling the fuselage of the plane almost completely. "We see about tha'." He drew a parang from its bamboo sheath and took a step toward Cowan. In that instant, a woman screamed. Wildly, desperately, a cry of mortal anguish came from somewhere on shore!

Yosha stiffened, glancing back toward the aircraft hatchway, startled.

Steve Cowan lunged. He hit the Malay with his shoulder, toppling him over backward. Yosha swung but the plane was too small a space to effectively wield the machete-like parang and the blade scraped sparks along the aluminum skin of the craft. The tip hit a rib in the metalwork and the weapon jumped from his grip.

Yosha's big hand grabbed for the handle of the weapon, as his other clutched at Cowan's shirt front.

Cowan jerked back, tearing the thin garment from the grasping hand. Both men lunged to their feet. Steve Cowan, quicker in reaction, smashed his head forward into Yosha's face in a frantic "Liverpool kiss." Yosha stumbled back and Steve jerked at his bindings, growling in frustration and fear.

A cord parted as the Malay stood up. Cowan jerked and twisted, one hand coming loose just as Yosha rushed. Cowan lashed out with a right, his wrist still wrapped in hemp, and the blow set his adversary back, but it was weak, the wrist and hand still numb from being bound. Fighting for his life Cowan swung a wicked blow to the brute's middle. Then he lunged into the Malay, his fists slamming the big muscle-corded body.

Yosha flinched away, staggering across the cabin. Yet now he held the thick-bladed knife ready, his teeth bared in a grimace of ferocious hate. Then, his feet wide apart, he started creeping along the narrow cabin toward Cowan. Cornered, desperate, Cowan feinted a blow as the islander lunged. Risking everything, the American hurled himself against Yosha's shoulder, and thrown off balance, both men toppled through the open hatch and struck the water.

Down, down, down! Then, somehow, Cowan discovered he was free and began desperately to swim for shore with powerful strokes.

As Cowan's head broke the surface, he glanced back. The plane rode gracefully on the blue water, not far away. But with the woman's scream still ringing in his ears, Cowan made no move to find out what had become of Yosha. He continued to swim swiftly toward shore. In a short while Cowan reached the shallows and splashed to land. He crossed the beach at a run. When the jungle had closed around him he felt safe.

Moving swiftly and silently, he worked his way toward the rambling plantation house, stripping the remains of the rope from his wrists. He was unarmed, and none knew better than himself the foe he was facing.

Ahead of Cowan was the wall of the Port Captain's house, and in it an open French window. He crossed the garden swiftly, moving from one clump of shrubbery to the next. Flattened against the wall, he peered in.

Isola Mayne was standing by a table. Her dress was torn. Masses of red–gold hair had fallen about her shoulders. Yet despite these things, never before had Cowan seen a woman look so regal, so beautiful, so commanding.

"You tell me!" Besi John Mataga's voice carried a soft but deadly threat. "If you don't, we kill the maid. Your butler was a fool. He gave us no time to explain." He gestured at the body of a man which Cowan noticed, for the first time, lying in the shadows, near the wall. "I'll kill you or this woman if I have to. Now, where's your brother's safe? We know he has one. Tell us, and we'll let you go."

"So that's what this is about." Isola Mayne's voice was low, and it made Steve Cowan's nerves tingle. "You want the shipping list? And my butler was a traitor, too? Well, you'll never find the list because it isn't here."

Mataga's face flushed and his eyes glinted with anger. But he merely turned away.

"Go ahead!" he told his men. "We'll see if she's as brave as she pretends."

Isola Mayne's face paled. "You wouldn't dare," she said, but Steve Cowan detected the resolution draining from her voice, and he saw how her eyes widened with horror. The men with Besi John were savage beasts.

Leaning further, he could see the two men holding the maid, a native girl. They had bent her arms cruelly behind her back. The girl's face was white, but her eyes were fearless.

"Don't tell them!" she cried. "They'll kill us anyway."

"Shut up!" Mataga whirled and struck the girl viciously across the mouth.

Instantly, the room burst into a turmoil of action. Isola Mayne, seizing a paper knife, was around the table with a movement that took the renegade by surprise.

Only a quick leap got him away from the knife. Then he caught the wrist of the actress and with a brutal wrench, twisted her to her knees.

In the same instant that Isola moved, Steve Cowan had plunged through the door. He hit the room running. The nearest of the men holding the maid dropped her arm and wheeled to face him, grabbing for his gun, but he was too slow.

Cowan went at him with a roundhouse swing that started at the door. It knocked the fellow sprawling into a corner, his face pulped and bloody. Springing across the fallen chair, Cowan leaped to close quarters with the other man. A shot blazed in his face, then the American's fist drove deep into the softness of the man's body, and he saw the fellow's face turn sick.

Someone jumped on him from behind. Dropping to one knee he hurled the man over his shoulder, then lunged to his feet just as Besi John Mataga whipped out a gun.

For a second Steve looked straight into the gun barrel. Lifting his eyes he could see death in Mataga's cruel face.

Then Isola Mayne twisted suddenly on the floor and kicked out with all her strength. At the same moment Mataga's pistol roared but the bullet went wild. Cowan moved. He hit Mataga in a sudden lunge and Mataga fell, cursing viciously.

Catching Isola's wrist, Cowan lifted her from the floor, and seizing the automatic from the table where it had fallen, charged for the door and the maid came stumbling after them.

How they reached the jungle, Steve Cowan never knew. He was aware of moving swiftly, of Isola beside him. When the maid stumbled and fell, he picked her up, almost collapsing after going the last few feet into the jungle. There had been shooting. He distinctly remembered the ugly bark of guns and the white lash of a bullet scar across a tree trunk ahead of him.

"Put me down." The voice brought him back to awareness. It was the maid speaking. He put her down carefully. Her face was white and set, but she seemed uninjured.

Isola was beside her in an instant. "Are you all right, Clara? If anything happens to you here, I'd never forgive myself."

"I'm all right."

Steve Cowan liked the blaze in her eyes. She wasn't afraid, only angry. His eyes went to Isola.

"I'm Steve Cowan," he said. Briefly, he explained. "What we'll do now," he added, "is anybody's guess. We'll have to keep moving until we find a place to hole up. Mataga won't quit. Especially," he added grimly, "now that I'm free."

"You knew him before?" Isola said. Her eyes flashed. "He's a spy."

"Two years ago we had difficulties on Siberut, an island near Sumatra."

They walked on in silence. Despite the maid's injured ankle and knee, he kept them moving along. There was no time for hesitation, Besi John would work swiftly and shrewdly.

Cowan studied the situation. It could hardly be worse. Esteville would not help him. Nominally the French were in charge, and no American Army officials could interfere without disclosing Cowan's true status. Whatever was done he must do himself. He checked the magazine of the automatic. Five shots remaining.

"We've got to recapture my plane," said Cowan. "Then I can fly you to Paagumene Bay." He looked at Isola. "Your butler was a traitor? He was selling you out to the Japs?"

"I guess so," answered the girl. "He'd

been with us for years and we trusted him. Oh, it's so horrible!"

They reached the edge of the jungle near where the plane was moored. A boat was alongside of the amphibian, and two Malays were seated in it with rifles across their knees. Another one of Besi John's men was standing in the cabin doorway.

"Well," Isola said, "it was a good idea."

Grimly Cowan sized up the situation. Three men with rifles. That chance was eliminated. They found a hollow beneath the roots of a giant ficus tree. It was dark, almost a cave. Cowan handed the automatic to Isola. "You may need this," he said. "What I have to do, it's best to do quietly."

She did not warn him, she did not suggest that he guard himself, but something in her eyes carried a tender message. For an instant her hand was on his arm as she smiled.

"Don't worry about us," she said.

•   •   •

Steve Cowan moved swiftly. He knew the jungle too well to be fearful. Even less than Besi John's imported Malays did he fear the abysmal darkness under the mighty trees. He was familiar with darkness; they superstitiously distrusted it.

There was, he recalled, a radio at the plantation. Since M. Esteville would not help him, he would help himself.

Night had fallen. Yet moving through the blackness under the trees, Steve Cowan knew it would be a help rather than otherwise. He left the jungle, and slipped swiftly from tree to tree across the lawn near the mansion.

The radio room was on the second story. He heard the murmur of voices inside. Then a guard walked along the porch near the railing. Behind the guard was the lattice he intended to use to get to the second floor. He could have waited, but impatience and hot, goading temper drove him on.

The guard, warned by some sixth sense, turned, and Cowan struck like a panther. His left smashed into the man's windpipe, knocking him gasping against the rail. Then the American chopped him across the eyes with the edge of his hand.

The man fell facedown on the porch, and did not move. His gun had fallen over the rail, but he wore a knife. With the blade in his teeth, Steve Cowan went up the lattice. A man sat at the radio, reading a magazine. Being here, he could only be a Mataga man.

Cowan slid a forearm under the man's chin, and crushed it against his windpipe. Then with a quick jerk, he wrenched the fellow back over his chair. Dragging him to the floor, Cowan spoke softly.

"Lie still and live," he said. "Move and you die."

He reached for a rope, and the native acted. He hurled himself at Cowan, his lips twisted in a snarl. Cowan's knife blade, held low and flat side down, slashed suddenly. Blood cascaded down the man's shirt front, and he slumped to the floor.

Cowan sat down at the radio. For an instant he held the key, then he began to send.

BENTON HARBOR . . . SS. BENTON HARBOR . . . NEW PLAN . . . COME AT ONCE.

KOYAMA.

A door swung open and another man appeared. Evidently he was another guard for he uttered a loud shout when he caught sight of Cowan. Then without hesitation he whipped out a gun and fired at the American. The sound of the shot rocked the building, and before the Malay could pull the trigger again, the American threw the knife—low and hard!

It struck! Horrified, the Malay stared at

the haft protruding from his stomach. The muzzle of his own weapon sagged as he reached for the knife and tugged it out. Blood gushed, and he fell.

Cowan caught up the gun and sprang into the hall. Two men were charging up the stairs and he sent slugs whizzing at them. Somehow he missed, so he dodged across the hall into another room, slamming the door after him. Then, crouching, he wheeled as bodies smashed against the door. He fired again, once, twice, until the gun clicked empty, and he dropped the useless weapon.

A noise behind him made Cowan turn quickly. A man had come into the window by means of the vines, and Cowan recognized him at once. It was Yosha, the bloodthirsty Malay who had tried to kill him on the amphibian.

Yosha looked bigger than ever. With bared teeth, he leaped at the American. Cowan's jab missed and he was seized by powerful arms, swept from his feet and hurled across the room. He hit the wall with a crash but came back fighting, although half stunned.

The Malay met the American with a straight arm and flung him against the wall once more. When Cowan tried a flying tackle, Yosha met it with a smashing knee that knocked him rolling to the floor. A kick to the forehead sent darts of pain lancing through his brain. The Malay was adept in this kind of fighting.

Drunk with agony, Cowan staggered to his feet. He had realized that this battle must be to the death. So he cut loose a terrific left hook which caught Yosha on the chin and rocked him to the heels. But the Malay only snarled, shook his head and replied with a bludgeoning blow which slashed Cowan across the cheek. Dazed, the American could not avoid the instant attack which followed.

Coolly, but with diabolical fury, the Malay tried to beat him into submission. Yosha had a knife in his belt and evidently meant to use it when he had punished the American to his satisfaction. But Cowan kept his head. He weathered the storm and continued to watch for his opportunity.

At last it came. As the knife flashed out Cowan tried another judo trick. Stepping in, he avoided the thrust, and flipped the blade inward. At the same moment he tripped Yosha. The Malay fell to the floor on top of the knife and rolled over. The knife was sticking out of his chest.

At this instant shots rang out in the direction of the beach. Cowan sprang for the window. He could see stabs of flame as more shots ripped the air. Still dizzy from the pounding he had received, the American cleared the sill and went down the vines outside.

Just what was happening he had no idea, but whatever the diversion, he must make it work to his advantage. Running swiftly, he headed for the woods.

• • •

The rattle of rifle fire down along the beach was growing. He swung away from that direction, cutting deeper into the jungle. Then he reached the ficus. Isola Mayne and the maid were gone!

Shocked, Steve Cowan froze, trying to understand. Isola would not have moved willingly, he knew that. The knowledge was no help. He started for the beach, moving fast.

The sound of firing had ceased. He slipped noiselessly through the jungle, and stared out. All was blackness beyond the edge of the trees and he could see nothing. He moved out, creeping slowly. Then he tripped and almost fell. He put his hand down. A dead man.

Feeling around in the dark he found a pistol, which he tucked into his belt, and moved on. His eyes grew accustomed to the darkness, and he saw more bodies.

There were corpses of white men among them, white men garbed as sailors.

Whatever the cause of the fight, it had been desperate. Out across the water he caught the outline of a Samson post against the sky. Then he knew.

The only ship in the Paagumene Bay with Samson posts had been the *Benton Harbor*. That meant Cowan's ruse to make Meyer betray himself had been successful. Peter Meyer had received his message.

Meyer, obviously, had been close by. That told Cowan that he had surmised the double cross Besi John Mataga had planned. Meyer's arrival had precipitated a battle.

One of Mataga's sentries must have fired on the ship, and Meyer, fearing a trap, had responded.

Steve Cowan stopped. What now? True, Meyer and Mataga were fighting, but that still didn't help him. The shipload of chrome would be moving out, and the

Japanese master spy, Koyama, was still loose. Also Isola Mayne was gone.

Nothing was settled, nothing was improved. He was free, but apparently helpless. Then he recalled the vague, misty dream of his flight to Oland Point, when he had been a prisoner aboard the plane. How long had they been in the air? He had no way of knowing, but he recalled the camel's hump, and the dark sky.

The dark hump . . . *Neangambo!*

He knew then. A Japanese submarine had surfaced in Nehue Bay. Neangambo was an island in the bay, and the dark hump of the hill and trees could be nowhere else near here. It must be the ship that had brought Koyama.

He worked his way along the shore to the edge of a village and as he had hoped, he found a catamaran. He shoved off and after a moment was alone, and slipping across the dark waters.

•   •   •

It was almost daylight when Steve Cowan, drunk with fatigue and his head throbbing with pain from the beating he had taken earlier, reached the shore opposite Neangambo.

The ship he had seen leaving Oland Point, the *Benton Harbor,* was there, and not far away, moored to a piling, was his own plane!

Steve Cowan wet his parched lips. All right, this was it. It was the work of minutes to bring the catamaran alongside the *Benton Harbor*. He paddled around to the bow, moored the boat to the anchor chain, and went up, hand over hand, at the risk of crushed fingers.

The deck was dark and still. He moved aft, slowly. Voices came from the saloon port. He slipped closer, then glanced in.

Peter Meyer, his face sour, sat at one end of the table. Nearby, her hands tied, was Isola Mayne. Behind her was the maid. Koyama sat with his back to the port, and across from him was Besi John Mataga, his face dark with fury.

"So?" Koyama's voice was sibilant. "You thought to betray us. Explain this, if you will."

Besi John laughed harshly. "Don't blame me for that. It was Cowan's work." He looked at the stout shipmaster. "Steuben, I think Cowan knew about what happened. You may resemble Meyer enough to fool some, Herman, but you didn't fool everyone!"

The thin Japanese officer, Koyama, made a gesture of impatience.

"All this is beside the point," he hissed. "Why did you kill our agent, the butler? The Burma man was valuable."

"I tell you I didn't know about it," shouted Besi John, angrily.

The Japanese master spy's anger increased. "You are a fool!" he snapped. "For that you will die." He waved his hand toward the women. "They must die, too. No one who knows our plans must remain alive."

Another voice, suave and smooth, broke in. "You must not do this, Commander Koyama. Miss Mayne is a famous actress, internationally known. She cannot disappear without causing complications. Better turn her over to my authority. I think I can make her see reason."

Esteville! The Frenchman was in this with them. All of which explained why the substitution of Steuben for Peter Meyer had been successful. Without hesitation Steve Cowan turned and walked into the cabin.

Mataga saw Cowan first. Trapped and in danger of losing his life, the renegade had been waiting for a chance to escape from the ship. Like a flash he leaped from his chair, darted through another door and disappeared. A loud splash revealed he had gone over the side.

Steve Cowan was too busy to follow. As Koyama lunged to his feet and whipped out a gun, Cowan raised his automatic and fired twice.

The Japanese officer's face turned sick, and he fell face forward across the table, dead.

It had happened so suddenly that it was like a slow-motion picture, but almost at once the saloon blazed with shots. Steuben grabbed for his gun, and lunged to his feet, firing desperately. Esteville crouched down, out of sight.

In a haze of powder smoke, Cowan saw Isola and the maid slip out of the door through which Besi John Mataga had disappeared. Steuben was down beside Koyama, now, the smoking pistol clutched in his lifeless fingers. Esteville was hiding behind a table. He had taken no part in the fight and there was no use remaining here any longer. Outside the crew had begun to shout and feet were approaching. So Cowan leaped through the doorway after the two girls, joining them at the railing.

A sailor, in plain sight, opened up with a rifle and Cowan knocked him spinning with one shot. Then with bullets from other members of the crew pattering around him, he swung over the rail and dropped Isola and the maid into the water near the catamaran.

More shots rang out and bullets snipped the water near the slim craft. Luckily the light, just before daylight, was not good, or they would have been slain. He continued to paddle furiously. Soon the freighter was out of sight and the firing stopped.

The plane was ahead, and Steve Cowan swung in close, then crawled aboard. He helped the girls into the cabin and slid into place behind the controls. After several attempts, he got the motors started and warmed them up.

When the ship was in the air, he took stock. The freighter below was moving now. They would get out, and get away fast. Soon Cowan noted two other freighters moving. A convoy, ostensibly bound for America, but, in reality, bound for Japan. The traitorous Pierre Esteville had made this possible.

But even well-laid plans can fail. Cowan swung his ship, and went down in a ringing, whistling dive. Then he opened up with the machine guns. His heavy projectiles blasted the bridge and ripped away the pilothouse windows. The freighter swung suddenly, and turned broadside to the channel.

Banking the Widgeon, Cowan swooped again. From stem to stern he plastered the freighters with gunfire. Then Isola screamed.

Cowan turned in his seat, startled. Besi John Mataga was standing in the middle of the amphibian's cabin, the small hatch to the bomb bay swinging on its hinges. As Cowan slid out of the seat and faced him, he sprang.

There was no choice but to fight, so Cowan met the renegade's rush. He got in one well-placed punch before Mataga closed with him, and the plane dipped dangerously.

Then they were locked in a furious, bitter fight. The plane was forgotten, there was no time to think, to reason, only to act. Slugging like a madman, he broke away from those powerful, clutching fingers. He smashed a left to Besi John's face, then a right to the windpipe. Mataga gasped, and sat down, then lunged and tackled Cowan and they both fell.

Through a haze of blood, Steve Cowan saw Isola had taken the controls. Then the renegade lunged for him, knife in hand. Slapping the wrist aside with his left, Cowan grasped it in his right hand, then thrust his left leg across in front of

Mataga's and his left arm over and under Mataga's right. He pressed down, and the half-caste screamed as his arm broke at the elbow, and his body lifted and arched, flying over the American's hip.

The right door had been knocked open, and the maid had been trying, vainly, to get it closed. Besi John's body caught in the doorway and then slipped through. He grabbed at the sill, desperately, and his fingers held for one breathtaking moment.

With a kind of dull horror, Steve Cowan saw Mataga tumbling down, down, down toward the waters of the bay. When he hit, a fleck of white showed, and he was gone.

Cowan turned, drunk with fatigue and punishment. Isola, her hair free in the wind from the open door, was flying the plane. She looked up at him suddenly, and smiled.

He looked down. A long, slim destroyer was sliding past Neangambo

Island. Another was off Tonnerre Point in the distance. Evidently the situation was under control.

He collapsed, suddenly, upon the floor.

When he opened his eyes, the ship was resting easily on the water. He looked up. An officer in the blue and gold of the Navy was standing over him.

"All right, old man?" the officer asked, grinning. "You had a rough time of it. We had been checking Esteville, and were suspicious of Meyer. We have him—all of them—in custody."

Steve Cowan looked up. Isola. He had been wondering whose shoulder his head was lying on.

"Then," he said, still looking at her, "I guess everything is under control."

The naval officer straightened. He smiled. The Navy knows something of women.

"Yes," he said thoughtfully, "I'd say it was."

BACKFIELD
BATTERING RAM

Leaning on the back of the players' bench, "Socks" Barnaby stared cynically at the squad of husky young men going through their paces on the playing field.

"You've got plenty of beef, Coach," he drawled, "but have you got any brains out there?"

Horace Temple, head coach at Eastern, directed a poisonous glare at the lean, broad-shouldered Barnaby, editor of the campus newspaper.

"What d'you care, Socks?" he said.

"Aren't you one of these guys who thinks football is overemphasized?"

"Me? I only think you've placed too much emphasis on sheer bulk. You need some smarts out there, that's all."

"Yeah?" The coach laughed. "Why don't you come out then? You were good enough at track and field last year."

"I haven't got the time."

"Crabapples!" Temple scoffed. "You've got time for more activities and fewer classes than any man on the campus. Editor of that scurvy sheet, president of the Drama Club, Poetry society . . . Writing that thesis on something or other is the only thing that keeps you from graduating!"

Coach Temple glanced back at the football field, and instantly he sprang to his feet.

"Kulowski!" he called. "What's the matter with you? Can't you even *hold* a football?" He glared at the lumbering bulk of "Muggs" Kulowski. "Of all the dumb clucks! Kulowski, get off the field. When you aren't fumbling, you're falling over one of my best men and crippling him. Go on, beat it!"

Muggs Kulowski looked up, his eyes pleading, but there was no mercy in Temple now. Slowly, his head hanging, Muggs turned toward the field house.

"That guy!" Coach Temple stared after him. "The biggest man I've got. Strong as an ox, an' twice as dumb. We're going to get killed this year!"

Thoughtfully, Barnaby stared after Kulowski. The man was big. He weighed at least forty pounds over two hundred, and was inches taller than Socks himself. But despite his size there was a certain unconscious rhythm in his movements. Still, in three weeks he hadn't learned to do anything right. For all his great size,

Kulowski went into a line as if he was afraid he'd break something, and his fingers were all thumbs.

"You cut us a break, Barnaby. All you do is use that sheet of yours to needle everybody who tries to do anything. A lot you've done for Eastern."

Socks grinned. "Wait until after the Hanover game," he said. "I'm just trying to save you from yourself, Coach. If you get by Hanover, we'll say something nice. I'd like to be optimistic but I've got to call it as I see it."

Barnaby walked off the field, heading for the quad. Kulowski was shambling along ahead of him, and something in the disconsolate appearance of the huge Pole touched a sympathetic chord in him. More, he was curious. It seemed impossible that any man with all his fingers could be as clumsy as this one. Stretching his long legs, Socks Barnaby quickened his pace to catch up with Kulowski.

"Hey, Kulowski, rough going today?" he asked, walking up beside the big fellow.

"Yeah." Muggs looked at him, surprised. "Didn't know you knew me."

"Sure," Socks replied. "Don't let this get you down. Tomorrow you'll do better."

"No," Muggs said bitterly. "He told me yesterday that if I messed up one more time I was through."

"Can't you get the hang of it?"

"No." The guy's brow furrowed. "I don't know what's wrong."

"Well, football isn't everything."

"For me it is," Kulowski said bitterly. "If I lose my scholarship, I'm finished. And I want a degree."

"That's something," Barnaby agreed. "Most football players don't care much about finishing. They just want to play ball. But if you lose the scholarship you can always get a job."

"I've got a job, but the money has to go home." He glanced at Socks. "I've got a mother, two sisters, and a kid brother."

Barnaby left Kulowski at the field house and started across the campus to the *Lantern* office in the Press Building. He was turning up the walk when he saw Professor Hazelton, and he stopped. The two were old friends, and Barnaby had corrected papers for him a few times, and written reviews for a book page the professor edited.

"Prof, don't you have Muggs Kulowski in a couple of classes?"

"Yes, of course. Why do you ask?" Hazelton was a slim, erect man of thirty-five and had been a crack basketballer.

"An idea I've got. Tell me about him."

"Well," Hazelton thought for a moment. "He always gets passing grades. He's not brilliant, mostly a successful plodder."

"How about recitations?" Barnaby asked.

"Very inferior. If it wasn't for his paper work he wouldn't get by. He's almost incoherent, although I must say he's shown some improvement lately."

After a few minutes, Socks Barnaby walked on into the office. He sat down at the typewriter and banged away on a story for the *Lantern*. It was several hours later, as he was finishing a letter to a girl in Cedar Rapids, when he remembered that Kulowski was working at the freight docks. On an inspiration, he got up and went out.

He liked Coach Temple. He and the coach had an old-time feud, but underneath there was a good deal of respect. Knowing a good many of the faculty and alumni, Barnaby had heard the gossip about the coach being on his last legs at Eastern. He had to turn out a team this year or lose his contract.

The fault wasn't wholly Temple's.

Other schools had more money to spend, and were spending it. Yet, here at Eastern, they expected Temple to turn out teams as good as the bigger, better financed schools.

Temple had a strategy. Digging around in the coal mines and lumber camps he had found a lot of huskies who liked the game, and many of them had played in high school and the Army. He recruited all he could but the teams he fielded were often uneven. This time it was his backfield where the weakness lay. They lacked a hard-hitting offensive combination. Kuttner was a good steady man, strong on the defense, and a fair passer and kicker. Ryan and DeVries were both fast, and fair backs, but neither of them was good enough to buck the big fast men that Hanover and State would have.

The freight dock was dimly lit and smelled of fresh lumber, tar, and onions.

Socks walked out on the dock and looked around. Then he saw Kulowski.

The big fellow hadn't noticed him. In overalls and without a shirt, with shoulders and arms that looked like a heavyweight wrestler's, he trundled his truck up to a huge barrel, tipped the barrel and slid the truck underneath, dipped the truck deftly, and started off toward the dim end of the dock.

Socks walked after him, watching. There was no uncertainty in Muggs Kulowski now. Alone here in the half-light of the freight dock, doing something he had done for months, he was deft, sure, and capable.

"Hi, Muggs," Socks said. "Looks like you're working hard." Kulowski turned, showing his surprise.

"Gosh, how did you happen to come down here?" he asked.

"Came to see you," Socks said casually. "I think we should get together on this football business."

Kulowski flushed. "Aw, I'm just no good. Can't get it through my head. Anyway, Coach is dead set against me."

"D'you play any other games?" Socks asked.

"Not exactly." Kulowski stopped, wiping the sweat from his face. "I used to play a little golf. Never played with anybody, just by myself."

"Why not?"

"I guess I wasn't good enough. I could do all right alone, but whenever anybody got around, I just couldn't hit the ball. I couldn't do anything."

Socks sat around the dock, strolled after Kulowski as he worked, and talked with the big fellow. Mostly, he watched him. The big guy was doing a job he knew. He was not conscious of being observed, and as he worked swiftly and surely, there wasn't a clumsy or awkward thing about him.

"I had trouble with games ever since I was a kid," Muggs Kulowski admitted finally. "My old man used to say I was too big and too awkward, and he made fun of me. I guess I was clumsy, growing fast and all."

"Muggs." Socks stood up suddenly. "We need you out there on that field this year. We need you badly. You know where Springer's barn is?"

"You mean that old red barn out there by the creek?"

"That's it. You meet me out there to-morrow. Bring your football suit, and don't tell anybody where you're going. We're going to work out a little."

They settled the time, and then Socks walked back to his room. He knew what it meant to grow fast and be awkward. His own father had been understanding, and had helped him get by that awkward period. But he knew how shy he had been himself, how it embarrassed him so terribly when anyone had laughed.

•   •   •

Socks, in a faded green sweater and slacks, walked out on the field the next afternoon. He paced off a hundred yards, and then walked back to the cottonwoods that divided the field from the edge of the campus. In a few minutes he saw Muggs, big as a house, coming up, grinning.

"Hi, Coach!" Muggs said. "What do I do first?"

"First we try you for speed," Socks said. "No use fooling with you if you're slow." He pointed. "See that stake down there? That's an even hundred yards. You go down there, and when I give you the word, shag it up here as fast as you can."

Muggs shambled down the field, turned and crouched in a starting position. At the barked command, he lunged forward.

Socks clicked the stopwatch as Muggs thundered past him, and looked thoughtful. Thirteen seconds, and there was a lot Kulowski didn't know about starting.

Barnaby dug out the football from his bag of gear.

He walked over to his pupil.

"You've got big hands," he said, "and long fingers, which is all to the good. But when you take hold of the ball, grip the thing, don't just let it lay in your hand. Take it between the thumb and fingers, with the fingers along the laces, just back of the middle. Press it well down into your hand with your left. When you pass, throw it overhand, right off the ear. You know all this, but we're going to work on it until it's automatic . . . until you can do it whether you're self-conscious or not."

It was almost dark when they left the field. For two hours Kulowski had practiced passing and receiving passes, and he had fallen on the ball until he seemed to have flattened every bit of grass on the field. They walked back toward the field house together, weary but cheerful.

"You'll do," Socks said quietly. "Don't let anything Coach said bother you.

You're big and you're fast. We'll have you faster. All you need is confidence, and to get over being afraid of other people looking on."

Muggs looked at him curiously.

"How come you aren't playing football?" he asked. "You seem to know plenty about it."

"Too many other things, I guess." Socks shrugged. "A man can't do everything."

The Hanover game was three weeks away. Sitting beside Muggs in the stands, Socks saw Eastern outplayed by Pentland, a smaller and inferior team.

It had been pretty bad. Socks glanced at Temple's face as the big coach lumbered off the field, and he didn't have the heart to rib him. Kuttner, battered from sixty minutes of play, looked pale and drawn.

One thing was sure, Socks decided. Hanover or State would ruin them. Hanover had an aerial game that was good, and as strong a line as Eastern's. Unless something happened to develop a behind-the-line combination for Eastern, an awful drubbing was in the cards.

Day after day, Barnaby met Kulowski in the field by the red barn, and worked the big guy and himself to exhaustion. Kulowski grinned when he got on the scales. His big brown face was drawn hard. He had lost almost twenty pounds in three weeks of work.

"Well, the Hanover game is tomorrow," Socks said, watching Kulowski curiously.

"What d'you think? Want to try it if the coach says yes?"

Kulowski's tongue touched his lips. "Yeah, I'll try," he said. "I can't do any more than mess it up."

"You won't mess it up. You're plenty fast now. You've cut two seconds off that hundred. And you know how to use your hands and your feet. If you get out there, just forget about that crowd. Just remember what we've been doing here, and do the same things."

Kulowski hesitated, staring at Barnaby, one of the most popular men in school. In those three weeks of bitter work, he had come to know him, to like him, and to respect him. He had seen that lean body lash out in a tackle that jarred every bone in his huge body. He had seen passes rifle down the field like bullets, right into his waiting arms.

Time and again Kulowski had missed those passes. They had slipped away, or dropped from his clumsy fingers, yet Socks had never been angry. He had kidded about it in friendly fashion, and encouraged him, flattered him.

Now, Kulowski wasn't missing the passes. He was taking kicks and coming down the field, and fast. Socks had shown him how to get to full speed at once, how to get the drive into his powerful legs. He had shown him how to tackle. He had taught him to use his feet and his hands.

For the first time, Kulowski felt that somebody believed in him, that somebody really thought he could do something without making a mess of it. Taunted and tormented so long for his size and awkwardness, Muggs had never known what it meant to be encouraged.

On his end, Socks knew that he had actually done little. Kulowski was a natural. All he had ever lacked was confidence. He liked doing things. He was big, and he was rough. Once confidence came to him, he threw himself into the practice with a will, his movements, day by day, became more sharp, more sure.

Socks stopped Coach Temple outside the field house. "Hi, Coach," he said grinning. "Why so glum?"

Temple scowled. "You trying to irritate

me? How would you feel going into that Hanover game without anything good in the backfield but Kuttner? They'll beat our ears off!"

"Can I quote you on that?"

"No!"

Socks dodged playfully backward as Temple rounded on him. "Are you willing to take a chance, Coach?"

"What d'you mean?"

"Put Kulowski in there, at half."

"Kulowski?" Temple exploded. "Are you crazy? Why, that big ox—"

"I said it was a chance," Socks interrupted. "But I've been working with him, and that boy is good."

"*You've* been working with him? What do you know about football?" Temple sneered, yet in the back of his eyes there was a hopeful, calculating expression.

"I read a book once." Socks grinned. "Anyway, what have you got to lose?"

Temple shrugged. "You got something there," he said wryly. "What?"

•   •   •

The stadium was jammed when the team trotted out on the field. Sitting on the bench beside Muggs Kulowski, Socks Barnaby talked to him quietly.

"This crowd is so big, it's impersonal. You just go out there and play a careful, steady game. You'll have your chance, and if you make good, you're back in."

Barnaby knew the huge crowd of fans hadn't come to see Eastern. There was little hope after the Pentland game that Eastern could win, and playing in Hanover backfield was Pete Tarbell, two hundred pounds of dynamite and twice an All-American. Besides that, in the Hanover line were two tackles said to be likely prospects for the All-American this year, and there was Speed Burtson, at right half, a former high school flash, and one of the most talked-of players in the college game.

Hanover was a star-studded team. Looking at them thoughtfully, Socks found himself wondering if they weren't a little too star-studded. And he found his eyes going again and again to Tarbell in his red jersey. He had known Pete Tarbell and didn't like him.

Kuttner kicked off to Hanover and Burtson took the ball on his own twenty yard line and ran it back to the forty yard line before he was downed by DeVries. Then Hanover began to roll.

They came through Hunk Warren, big Eastern tackle, for two first downs. Then Tarbell came over guard for six. Tarbell tried Hunk again, but Kuttner came down fast and Tarbell was stopped dead. They passed on the third down.

The pass was good, plenty good. Speed Burtson, living up to his name, went down the field fast, evaded Kuttner, and took the pass over his shoulder. He went over into the end zone standing up for the first score. Tarbell kicked, and Hanover had a lead of seven to nothing.

The rest of the first quarter was murder.

Eastern could hold their opponents in the line, but the Hanover aerial attack was beyond them. Twice Burtson got away for long gains, and Tarbell came around the left end and crashed into DeVries, taking him over into the end zone with him. Hanover missed the kick, but when the play was over, DeVries was on the ground. He got up and limped off the field.

Coach Temple paled and he swore under his breath. He looked at Kulowski, then at Socks. "All right, Muggs," he said grimly. "You go in at full."

Ryan was at quarterback for Eastern, Kulowski at full, Kuttner at left halfback and Hansen at right half.

Socks glanced up at the stands. President Crandall was there, and the short, fat-jowled man beside him would be Erich P. Wells, head of the Alumni Association. Socks glanced at Temple and saw the big coach was kicking his toe into the turf, his face drawn. Temple had expected defeat, but this was going to be slaughter.

The tension was getting to him. Socks wanted Kulowski to do well but he didn't have a good feeling about this game. He slid off the bench and took a walk around the stands, he had another thought but it was crazy . . . the coach would laugh at him. . . .

When he got back, Temple glowered at Socks.

"Kulowski's fumbled once already," the coach growled. "Kuttner made a recovery."

Socks' heart sank. Eastern was lining up again. He could see the uncertainty in the big Pole. The ball was snapped and Kuttner started around the end. Kulowski came in, hurled himself halfheartedly at Tarbell's feet as the big back lunged through. Tarbell merely sidestepped neatly, then launched himself in a tackle that brought Kuttner down with a thud they could hear on the sidelines.

"I'm going to take that big lug out of there!" Temple barked. "He's yellow!"

"Let me go in," he suggested. "I can make him work."

Temple turned, staring.

"You, Socks? Where'd you ever play football?"

"I played against Tarbell," Socks said. "I was with the Gorman Air Base team."

Temple looked at him cynically. "Gorman Air Base, eh? You ain't lyin'? All right, Socks, but you aren't writing poetry out there. Suit up!"

When Socks trotted out on the field he suddenly felt as Kulowski must. It had been four years and when he looked at Hanover's big line, he felt his heart go down into his stomach. Those huge guards! And that center, as enormous as a concrete pillbox!

Then, behind the line, Socks saw big Pete Tarbell staring at him. Then the stare changed to a wolfish smile.

"Well, well!" he said, "if it isn't the

bomber boy. What do you think this is, badminton?"

Socks ignored him. He trotted up and grabbed Kulowski. "Listen," he said, "I'm here now, and I'm going to be playing with you. But you've got to focus . . . let's play this one just like out behind the barn. You can do it."

Kulowski flushed, "I'll try," he said.

"Crabapples!" Socks grinned. "Turn loose on these guys an' you can wreck that team. Let's go out there and bust 'em up!"

He trotted over to Ryan and whispered for a moment. Ryan nodded, looking doubtful.

"Okay," he said, "if Coach says so."

Kulowski took the ball. For a wonder, his big fingers clamped on it and he started moving. Behind him he heard Socks' voice and saw the lean redhead move in ahead of him. Hunk had a hole and Kulowski went through, his big knees lifting high.

Pete Tarbell saw him coming and angled over, but suddenly Socks knifed across and Tarbell hit the ground with a thud. He got up slowly, and looked at Barnaby.

"Hi," Socks said, grinning, "how's the badminton?"

Tarbell glowered and his face set. Kulowski had been downed on the thirty yard line. He had made six yards.

Kulowski got up grinning. It was the first successful thing he had ever accomplished in front of a crowd. He looked at Barnaby, and as Socks passed Ryan, Socks said, "Give it to Muggs again."

Ryan barked the signals. Muggs Kulowski took the ball running and hit the line hard. He went through for four yards. Kulowski was getting warmed up. Ryan worked Kuttner on a reverse and he got away for ten yards before he was downed.

Socks had thrown a wicked block into Burtson and as he got up he saw Tarbell rising shakily from the ground and glowering at Kulowski. The big Pole was grinning from ear to ear.

The Eastern team was working now. Kulowski's face was sweat streaked and muddy, but he was still grinning. He was hitting that line with power and whenever he hit, something happened. He wasn't missing any passes, and all the fear of the crowd, the fear of being laughed at was gone. He was in there, driving, and his two hundred and twenty pounds was making itself felt.

Eastern worked smoothly and marched down the field. They got to the thirty, and there Hanover smashed them back three times. Hanover was concentrating on Kulowski now, sensing his power and drive.

"You think we ought to pass it?" Ryan whispered to Socks.

"Yeah." Socks glanced around. "Give it to me in the corner."

Socks Barnaby slid around end and went down the field fast and took the ball on the three. There Tarbell hit him like a tank, and Socks went down and rolled over. Tarbell got up.

Ryan called for Kulowski. The big Pole tucked the ball under his arm and put his head down and drove. The Hanover line bulged, and then it gave way all of a sudden. Kulowski powered through, and they had the score.

Socks dropped back and kicked the point. The score was 13 and 7 at the half.

To open the second half it was Hanover's choice, and they elected to receive. Kuttner toed the ball. Ammons, Hanover's big right tackle, took it coming fast, but Kulowski was moving and he drove the bigger Ammons back on his shoulder.

Hanover lined up, Tarbell came plunging through, and Kulowski hit him.

Tarbell got slowly to his feet, and he looked wonderingly at the big guy. Tarbell, twice All-American, had lost a yard on the play!

Tarbell came in again like a battering ram and there was murder in his drive. Hunk was ready this time and he hit Tarbell at the knees, then Kulowski hit him high, and Tarbell went down, hard.

Tarbell had lost two yards, and he was mad clear through. Socks ran back to position, laughing at the puzzled, angry face of the Hanover star.

Then Hanover got tough. Eastern drove at the line three times and made only three yards.

Burtson kicked. He lived up to reputation, booting a low whirler that hit and rolled over and over. The wind helped it, but Socks finally downed the ball on the Eastern sixteen.

They made three first downs, then Hanover got hot and swamped them. Taking Kuttner's kick, Hanover began to hammer. They sent Tarbell through the line, and ganged Hunk Warren to make the hole. They made it. Tarbell came through, his head down, driving like a locomotive, but Muggs Kulowski was coming in. He had an urge to ruin Tarbell and they both knew it. They hit hard and bounced apart, both of them shaken to the heels.

Eastern took possession of the ball on downs and powered it straight down the field as the quarter neared its end. They got to the seven, and Kulowski had been doing most of the work. Socks took the ball off tackle with Kulowski and Ryan clearing the way, and went over the line standing up.

Kuttner missed the point and the score was tied.

The last quarter opened and the big Hanover team came out for blood. They were against a team that seemed to be playing way over its head, and it had Hanover desperate for fear the mounting confidence of Eastern would smear them.

Then it happened. It was Eastern's ball on their own forty yard line. Eastern lined up and Kulowski went off tackle for four. Then Kuttner started around the end, but Sinclair, a Hanover end, cut in for him, and with a quick shift, Kuttner went through the messup at guard, charging the center of the field.

A huge Hanover tackler missed him, got a hand on his leg, and Kuttner spun around, staggering three steps and then went down under a rib-cracking tackle from Speed Burtson.

They lined up and Ryan sent Kulowski

through the line for four. The big fellow got up, and he grinned at Socks.

"We're doin' it, boy!" he said. "This is fun!"

"We got a chance," Kuttner said. "We got a good chance. It's with you, Socks, or Kulowski."

"It's Kulowski," Socks said. "Listen, Muggs. Remember those long passes out there by the creek? You get away this time and get off down the field, but fast. Go around the left end and when you get down there, angle across the field. Wherever you are, you'll get that pass."

Socks glanced at Ryan.

"Okay," he said. "Let's go!" He spun on his heel and said to Muggs, "All right, let's see the deer in those big feet of yours!"

The center snapped the ball back to Socks, and he dropped back for the pass. Kuttner started around the end, and Burtson, thinking the pass was for Kuttner, started after him. Ryan had gone through the middle, and suddenly, Socks, still falling back, saw Kulowski away off down the field. He was really running. It would be forty yards, at least.

As a big tackle lunged toward him, Socks shot the pass in a rifling spiral that traveled like a bullet, just out of reach of leaping hands. Then Kulowski went up, the ball momentarily slipped through his hands, and a terrific groan went up from the stands, but then he recovered and was running!

Tarbell had been playing far back, and he started slow as Kulowski came toward him. Then the big All-American's pace changed suddenly, his toes dug in and he hurled himself in a dynamite-charged tackle at Muggs.

Kulowski made a lightninglike cross step, and at the same moment, his open hand shot out in a wicked stiff-arm, backed by all the power of those freight-handling muscles. That hand flattened against Tarbell's face and the clutching hands grasped only air.

Two men got Kulowski on the two yard line, bringing him down with a bone-crushing jolt.

They lined up again, and Ryan looked at Muggs and Kulowski grinned. They snapped the ball, and he went through the middle with everything he could give. They tried to hold him, but for the first time in his life, Muggs Kulowski was playing with everything he had in him. He put his head down and drove.

With four men clinging to him, he shoved through. The ball was over.

The rest was anticlimax. Socks Barnaby dropped back and booted the ball through the goal posts, and the whistle blew.

It was 20 to 13!

"Well," Barnaby said to Temple as the big coach stood waiting for them, "what did I tell you?"

"You tell me?" The Coach grinned. "Why, I knew that you were all brains an' he was all beef. What d'you suppose I needled you for? Don't you suppose I knew that thesis of yours was on the sense of inferiority?"

"Crabapples!" Socks scoffed. "Why, you couldn't—!"

"Listen, pantywaist," Temple growled. "D'you suppose I'd ever have let you an' Muggs on that field if I didn't know you could do it? Don't you suppose I knew you an' him were down behind that red barn every night? What d'you suppose I kicked him off the field for? I knew you were so confounded contrary you'd get busy an' work with him just to show me up!"

"Well," Socks grinned, "it wasn't you who got showed up. It was Hanover."

"Yeah," Temple agreed, "so go put that in the *Lantern*. And you, Kulowski. You get out for practice, you hear?"

"Okay," Kulowski said. Then he grinned. "But first I got to write an article for the *Lantern*."

Coach Temple's eyes narrowed and his face grew brick red.

"You? Writing for the *Lantern*? What about?"

"Coaching methods at Eastern," Kulowski said, and laughed.

He was still laughing as he walked toward the field house with his arm across Barnaby's shoulders.

ANYTHING FOR A PAL

Tony Kinsella looked at his platinum wristwatch. Ten more minutes. Just ten minutes to go. It was all set. In ten minutes a young man would be standing on that corner under the streetlight. Doreen would come up, speak to him, and then step into the drugstore. Once Doreen had put the finger on him, confirming that he was, in fact, the man they sought, the car would slide up, and he, Tony Kinsella, Boss Cardoza's ace torpedo, would send a stream of copper-jacketed bullets into the kid's body. It would be all over then, and Tony Kinsella would have saved his pal from the chair.

He looked up to the driver's seat where "Gloves" McFadden slouched carelessly, waiting. He noted the thick neck, and heavy, prizefighter's shoulders. In the other front seat "Dopey" Wentz stared off into the night. Kinsella didn't like that. A guy on weed was undependable. Kinsella shrugged, he didn't like it but the whole mess would soon be over.

This kid, Robbins, his name was, he'd seen Corney Watson pull the Baronski job. Tomorrow he was to identify Corney in court. Corney Watson had sprung Kinsella out of a western pen one time, so they were pals. And Kinsella, whatever his failings, had one boast: he'd do anything for a pal. Tony was proud of that. He was a right guy.

But that was only one of the two things he was proud of. The other the boys didn't know about, except in a vague way. It was his brother, George. Their name wasn't Kinsella, and George had no idea that such a name even existed. Their real name was Bretherton, but when Tony had been arrested the first time, he gave his name as Kinsella, and so it had been for a dozen years now.

Tony was proud of George. George was ten years the youngest, and had no idea that his idolized big brother was a gangster, a killer. Tony rarely saw him, but he'd paid his way through college, and into a classy set of people. Tony smiled into the darkness. George Bretherton: now wasn't that a classy name? Maybe, when he'd put a few grand more in his sock, he'd chuck the rackets and take George off to Europe. Then he'd be Anthony Bretherton, wealthy and respected.

Kinsella leaned back against the cushions. This was one job he was pulling for nothing. Just for a pal. Corney had bumped "Baron" Baronski, and this kid had seen it. How he happened to be there, nobody knew or cared. Tomorrow he was going to testify, and that meant the chair for Corney unless Tony came through tonight, but Tony, who never failed when the chips were down, *would* come through.

They had located Robbins at a downtown hotel, a classy joint. Cardoza sent Doreen over there, and she got acquainted. Doreen was a swell kid, wore her clothes like a million, and she was wise. She had put the finger on more than one guy. This Robbins fellow, he wasn't one of Baronski's guns, so how had he been there at the time? Tony shrugged. Just one of those unfortunate things.

Why didn't George write, he wondered? He was working in a law office out west somewhere. Maybe he'd be the mouthpiece for some big corporation and make plenty of dough. That was the racket! No gang guns or coppers in that line, a safe bet.

Tony wondered what Corney was doing. Probably lying on his back in his cell hoping Kinsella would come through. Well, Tony smiled with satisfaction; he'd never botched a job yet.

Suddenly Dopey hissed: "Okay, Tony, there's the guy."

"You think! When you see Doreen comin', let me know. I'm not interested 'til then."

He suddenly found himself wishing it was over. He always felt like this at the last minute. Jumpy. Prizefighters felt that way before the bell. Nerves. But when the gun started to jump he was all right. He caressed the finned blue steel of the barrel lovingly.

"Get set, Tony, here she comes!" The powerful motor came to life, purring quietly.

Kinsella sat up and rolled down the window. The cool evening air breathed softly across his face. He looked up at the stars, and then glanced both ways, up and down the street. It was all clear.

A tall, broad-shouldered fellow stood on the corner. Tony could see Doreen coming. She was walking fast. Probably she was nervous too. That big guy. That would be him. Tony licked his lips and lifted the ugly black muzzle of the submachine gun. Its cold nose peered over the edge of the window. He saw a man walk out of the drugstore, light a cigar, and stroll off up the street. Tony almost laughed as he thought how funny it would be if he were to start shooting then, how startled that man would be!

There! Doreen was talking to the man on the corner. Had one hand on his sleeve . . . smiling at him.

God, dames were coldblooded! In a couple of minutes that guy would be kicking in his own gore, and she was putting him on the spot and smiling at him!

Suddenly she turned away and started for the drugstore on some excuse or other. As she passed through the door she was almost running. The car was moving swiftly now, gliding toward the curb, the man looked up, and the gun spouted fire. The man threw up his arms oddly, jerked sharply, and fell headlong. McFadden wheeled the car and they drove back, the machine gun spouting fire again. The body, like a sack of old clothes, jerked as the bullets struck.

The next morning Tony lay on his back staring at the ceiling. He wondered where Doreen was. Probably the papers were full of the Robbins killing. Slowly he crawled out of bed, drew on his robe, and retrieved the morning paper from his apartment door. His eyes sought the headliners, blaring across the top in bold type:

GANG GUNS SLAY FEDERAL OPERATIVE.
MACHINE GUNS GET WATSON WITNESS.

Tony's eyes narrowed. A federal man, eh? That wasn't so good. Who would have thought Robbins was a federal man? Still, they were never where you expected them to be. Probably he'd been working a case on Baronski when Corney bumped him off. That would be it.

His eyes skimmed the brief account of the killing. It was as usual. They had no adequate description of either Doreen or the car. Then his eyes glimpsed a word in the last paragraph that gripped his attention. His face tense, he read on.

Slowly, he looked up. His eyes were

blank. His face looked old and strained. Walking across to the table he picked up his heavy automatic, flipped down the safety, and still staring blankly before him, put the muzzle in his mouth and pulled the trigger.

His body toppled across the table, the blood slowly staining the crumpled paper and almost obliterating the account of the Robbins killing. The final words of the account were barely visible as the spreading stain wiped it out:

"A fact unknown until the killing was that Jack Robbins, witness for the prosecution in the Baronski killing, was in reality George Bretherton, a Federal operative recently arrived from the Pacific Coast and working on his first case. He is survived by a brother whose present whereabouts are unknown."

FROM THE
LISTENING HILLS

The hunted man lay behind a crude parapet in a low-roofed, wind-eroded cave on the north slope of Tokewanna Peak. One hundred yards down the slope, at an approximate altitude of eleven thousand feet, just inside a fringe of alpine fir, were scattered the hunting men.

The bare, intervening stretch of rock was flecked here and there with patches of snow. Within the fringe of trees but concealed from his view except for the faint wisps of smoke, were the fires of his pursuers.

Boone Tremayne had no fire, nor at this time dared he make one, for as yet his position was not exactly known to the armed men.

It was very cold and he lay on his stomach, favoring his left side where the first bullet had torn an ugly wound. The second bullet had gone through his thigh, but his crude bandages as well as the cold had caused the bleeding to stop.

A low wind moaned across the rock, stirring the icy bits of snow on the cold flanks of the peak which arose two thousand feet above and behind him. Within the low cave it was still light, and Boone Tremayne clutched the stub of pencil and looked down at the cheap tablet at his elbow.

He must write with care, for what he wrote now would be all his son, as yet unborn, would ever know of his father and uncles. He would hear the stories others would tell, and so it would be important for him to have some word in his father's hand.

The pencil clutched awkwardly in his chilled fingers, he began to write:

"It's getting mighty cold up here, Son, and my grub's about gone. My canteen's still half full, but it ain't no use, they've done got me.

"Time to time I can hear them down in the brush. There must be a hunert of them. Seems an awful lot of folks to git one lone man. If I only had Johnny here I wouldn't feel so bad. Johnny, he always sort of perked a feller up no matter how bad things got.

"Except for you, I'm the last of the Tremaynes. Somehow it ain't so lonely up here knowing there's to be a son of mine somewheres.

"Now, Son, your ma is a mighty good woman as well as a pretty one. I never figured, no way you look at it, to get such a girl as Marge. If she'd married up with Burt, or Elisha, I'd no-ways have blamed her. They were the pick of the lot, they were.

"Just had me a look down there an' I reckon they are gitting set to rush me. Wished they wouldn't. I never aimed to kill nobody. They figured to hang me if I'm got alive, and I promised Ma I'd never stretch no rope. Least a man can do is die with his face toward them who aims to kill him."

Boone Tremayne put down the stub of pencil and chafed his cold fingers, peering through the stacked flakes of rock he had heaped into a wall before the opening. The cold was all through him now, and he knew he would never be warm again. That was okay, he had this one last job to do . . . and then he no longer cared. The wind whispered to the snow and then he saw a man, bulky with a heavy coat, lunge from the trees and come forward in a stumbling run.

A second man started as the first dropped behind a shelf of rock, and Boone put his cheek against the cold stock of the Winchester and squeezed off his shot. He put the bullet through the man's leg, saw the leg buckle and saw the man fall. Another started and Boone dropped him with a bullet through the shoulder.

He gnawed at his lip and stared, hollow-eyed and gaunt, at the shelf of rock where the first man had fallen. "Reckon I'd best let you git cold, too, mister," he said, and flicked a glancing shot off the rock over the man's head. That would let him know he had been seen, that it would be dangerous to try moving.

He shifted his position, favoring his wounded side and leg. Nobody moved, and the afternoon was waning. At night they would probably come for him. He glanced at the sullen gray sky. There was still time.

"It started over a horse. We Tremaynes always found ourselves good horse flesh. Johnny, he ketched this black colt in the hills near Durango. Little beauty, he was, and Johnny learned him well and entered him in a race we always had down around there.

"Dick Watson, him and his brothers, they fancied horses too and one of Dick's horses had won that race four years running. We all bet a sight of money. Not so much, when you figure it, but a mighty lot for us, who never had much cash in hand. Johnny's black just ran off and left Watson's horse, and Watson was mighty put out.

"He said no horse like that ever run wild, and that Johnny must of stole him somewheres. Johnny said no he never and that Watson's horse just wasn't all that fast. Watson said that if Johnny wasn't such a boy, him being just sixteen, he'd whup him good. Then our brother Burt, he stepped up. Burt was a mighty big, fine figure of a man. He stepped up and said he wasn't no boy, if it was a fight Watson wanted.

"Well, Burt, he beat the tar out of Dick Watson. There was hard words said, and Ma, she reckoned we all better git for home. We did, an' everything went along for a time. Until that black was found dead. Somebody shot her down in the pasture. Shot her from clost up.

"Johnny, he was all for going to town and gitting him a man, but Ma, she said no and Burt and Lisha, they sided with her. But Johnny . . . well, it was some days for he tuned up that mouth organ of his. And when he done it, it was all sad music.

"We wasn't cattlemen, Son, not like other folks around. We was farmers and trappers, or bee hunters, anything there was to git the coon. Mostly, them days, we farmed and between crops we went back in the high meadows and rounded us up wild horses.

"They was thousands of them, Son. Land sakes, I wished you could of seen them run! It were a sight too beautiful for man to look upon. We rounded up a sight of them, but we never kept but a few. We'd pick the youngest and prettiest. We'd gentle them down with kindness and good grass and carrots, then we'd break them. My Pap, he broke horses for a gent in Kentucky, a long time ago and he knew a goer and a stayer. I guess none of us ever did forgit that little black mare.

"Now that horse was shot clost up. It was no accident. And no man would kill a good horse like that. Except for if he done it in pure meanness. And who had him a reason? Dick Watson. That black mare beat Watson's horse once and he would do it again. Johnny, he never said much, but from that day on he packed him a gun, and he never had afore.

"Them boys down in the bresh is fixing to move. Gitting cold I reckon."

Boone Tremayne's head throbbed with fever and he stared through the chinks in the flaked rock. The man under the ledge stirred cautiously and Boone put a shot down there to keep him from stretching out too much. He rubbed his hands and blew upon the fingers. A man moved in the brush and Boone laid a bullet in close to the ground.

Bullets hailed around his shelter, most of them glancing off the rocks, but one got inside and ricocheted past his head. A hair closer and he would have been dead.

Flat on his belly he stuffed the tablet and pencil in his pocket and crawled along the bottom of the shallow cave. Painfully, he wormed his way along the cave for thirty yards and found a place where it was a few inches deeper and where some animal or bird had long since gathered sticks for a nest or home. Gathering some of the dead sticks together, Boone built a fire.

The long-dead wood made little smoke and the tiny flame was comforting. Later, when it was dark the reflection would give him away so he tried to shield it with rocks as much as he could. He held his blue and shaking fingers almost in the flame, but it was a long time before any warmth reached him.

They were waiting now, waiting for darkness. He must finish his letter. There would be no time later.

"Mighty cold, Son, I've moved a mite and got me a fire. Well, the black was dead but we had us about forty head of good horses ready to move. Sam and Lisha, they set out for Durango. We figured to buy Ma a new dress for her birthday and to get us some tools we needed and other fixings. Going in the boys had to drive past the DW where the Watsons ranched. They seen Dick a-watching them, but thought nothing of that at the time.

"Well, when they got into Durango the sheriff come high-tailing it up with five, six men, all armed heavy. They tell the boys they are under arrest for stealing horses. The boys tell them they trained them horses, that they was wild stock afore. The sheriff and that bunch with him, one of them was a Watson, they just laughed.

"Well, the boys was throwed in jail, but the sheriff, he wouldn't let them get word to the rest of us. Only Johnny, he got to thinking and when the boys was slow gitting back, he mounts up and heads for town. But they was ready for him, the Watsons was.

"Johnny, he seen the horses in the corral, and he high-tails it for the sheriff. The sheriff is out of town, maybe a-purpose, and Johnny, he goes into the

T-Diamond Saloon. And there's three Watsons and two brothers-in-law of theirs, all setting around.

"These brothers-in-law, one named Ebberly, the other Boyd. This Boyd was some gun-slinger or had that reputation. Johnny, he never knowed them at all, but he knowed the Watsons. He asked the barkeep where was his brothers, and Dick Watson speaks up and says they are in jail for stealing horses, where he'll soon be. Johnny, he knows what Ma would say, and remarkable for him, keeps his head. He says nothing and turns to go and Dick Watson says, 'Like you stole that black mare.'

"The three Watsons are spread out and ready. He seen then it was a trap, but still he never knowed those other two which sat quiet near the door, never saying I, yes, or no. Johnny, he says, 'I trained that black mare, Watson, an' you kilt her. You snuck up an' shot that pore little horse dead.'

" 'I never!' Watson says, and folks say he looked mighty red in the face. 'You're a liar!'

"Watson grabbed iron and so did Johnny. The Watsons, they got three bullets into Johnny, but he still stood, so this Boyd, he shoots him in the back. Johnny went down, but there was two Watsons on the floor, one dead, and Dick badly hurt.

"Johnny, they figured for dead, and they was so busy gitting their kin to the doc they never thought of him. He was alive and he crawled out of there. A girl he knowed in town, she got her Pap, who was a vet, and he fixed Johnny up and hid him out.

"This here girl, she run down to the jail and told Lisha and Sam through the bars. She said they better get set, there'd be trouble. She had Johnny's gun and she passed it through the bars and along with it a chunk of pipe standing close by.

"We heard about it after. The one

Watson that was on his feet, him and Ebberly, Boyd and some half dozen others, they got them masks and come down to the jail to lynch the other boys. They got into the jail and the jailor he just stepped aside, easy as you please, and says, 'In the second cell.'

"They rushed up. The boys just stood a-waiting, just like they didn't know what was going to happen. The barred door swung open and then Lisha, he outs with his gun and that bunch scrambled, believe you me. One of them turns to slam shut the door, but Sam, he got his pipe betwixt the door and the jam to keep it from closing. That feller dragged iron, so Sam raised the pipe and shoved it into his throat. That feller went down. The mob beat it, and so the boys, they took out. They told that jailer they would surrender to a U.S. Marshal, but nobody else.

"Lisha and Sam, they went to the corral and got their horses, every head, and they started out of town. By that time the story got around that the Tremayne boys had killed two men and wounded a couple of others, then broke jail. So they fetched their guns and come running.

"They got Sam right off. Folks said he was shot nine times in that first volley. At that, Lisha rode back to pick him up, but he couldn't get nigh the body, and could see by the way Sam was that he must be dead. So he headed off to home with his horses."

Boone Tremayne put aside his letter and added a few tiny sticks to his little fire. It was so small a man might have held it in his two hands, but the little flame looked good, and it warmed his fingers which were cramped from writing and the cold.

An icy wind blew over the slope of the mountain. Boone looked longingly at the woods below, and the first silver line that was the Middle Fork of the Green, which stretched away almost due north from where he lay. If he could get down there he might still have a chance . . . but there was no chance. The lost blood, the lack of food and the cold had drawn upon his strength until he was only a dank shell of a man, huddled in his worn clothes, shivering and freezing and looking down at the hunters who held him.

Cautiously, the man under the shelf below was moving. He, too, was feeling the cold. "Well, feel it," Boone whispered, "maybe next time you won't be so anxious to go hunting a lone man!" He ricocheted another bullet off the rock shelf.

Several rifles replied, and suddenly angry, Boone fired a careful shot at the flash of one of the guns. He heard a rifle rattle on rocks as it fell, and then a heavy body tumbling into brush. More shots were fired, but now he had turned ugly, the loneliness, the cold, the fear of death, all crowded in upon him and he shot rapidly and frantically, at rifle flashes, and dusting the brush around the smoke of the fires. He fired his rifle empty and reloaded and then with careful shots, proceeded to weed the woods below.

Then he doused his fire and moved further along the undercut rock and found another place, almost as good as the last. Here he started another tiny blaze, shielding it with a large slab of flat rock.

"Finished off telling how Sam was kilt. Johnny, he was shot bad and we didn't know if he was dead for two days, then that girl, Ellie Winters, she come up the mountain with the news. The town was mighty wrought up. Some of them was coming up after us.

"We kept watch, Burt, Lisha and me. Meanwhile, we tried figuring what to do. For Ma's sake we would have to pull out, git up into the high meadows or west into the wild country over the Utah line.

"Now we knowed they was hunting Johnny, and Ellie's Pa was worried too. So the three of us ups and goes down to Durango. Johnny, he mounted the horse we brought for him, and we dusted out of there.

"Slow, and careful not to leave no tracks, we moved out, leaving our cabin, our crop, everything but the horses. We made it west-northwest past Lone Cone and finally crossing the San Miguel into Uncompahgre Plateau country. We found us a little box canyon there with grass and water, and we moved in. By hunting we made out, but Ma was feeling poorly so Burt, he stayed with her while Lisha and me, we mounted up and with five head of horses, we headed for a little town north of us on the river. We sold our horses, bought up supplies and come back.

"Ma, she didn't get no better, and finally, she died one morning, just died a-setting in her rocker. We'd brung that rocker along, and it had been a sight of comfort for her. So Ma died and Johnny played his mouth organ, and we buried her. Then there was just the four of us, with Johnny still recuperating from his bullet wounds.

"Them horses we sold let folks know where we was, and soon there was a posse after us. We were figured to be outlaws, real bad hombres. We'd killed folks and we'd busted jail. That posse cornered us in the mountains and we shot it out and got away.

"That began the bad and lonely time, made pleasant only because we were together. We drifted west into the La Balas and sold our horses except for an extry for each of us, and then drifted into the Robber's Roost country. It was there I kilt my first man. It was that there Boyd. The same one who shot Johnny in the back.

"He'd kilt a woman in Colorado, and then her man. After that the country got too hot to hold him so he drifted west to the Roost. There was a shack in the Roost them days, a log shack, long and low. The floor was adobe and there was a bar and a few tables. It was low-roofed, dark, and no ways pleasant. It was outside of that place I come up to Boyd.

"He seen me and he stopped. 'Another one of them miserable Tremaynes!' he sneers.

"Men stopped to listen and watch. 'You shot Johnny in the back,' I tell him, 'and I figure you're good for nothing else!' He grabs iron and about that time my gun bucks in my hand and this gent he just curls up and folds over.

"The boys come a-running and we look at that passel of rustlers, thieves and no accounts, with a few mighty good men scattered among them. 'Anybody got a argyment?' Burt asks.

"One gent, his name was Cassidy, he chuckles, and says, 'Boyd was no good and we knowed it. Anyway,' he grins at us, 'the weight o' the artillery is on your side!' Then he bought a round of drinks.

"We drifted north through Wyoming, selling a few horses we broke and working time to time on spreads in the Wind River and Powder River countries. We drifted north into Montanny, and finally down to Deadwood. Here and there we heard rumors. Folks said we were robbing banks and trains, which we never done. Folks said we had killed this man or that one, and without ever doing a thing, we got us a name 'most as bad as the James boys. All on account of how people love to talk and gossip.

"The fact that I killed Boyd got back to Colorado. He'd been some shakes as a gunman, so they now had me pegged as one. Boyd, I kilt, but if they figured he was fast, they wasn't figuring right. In Deadwood I heard Ebberly was in town, making his brags what he would do if he ever come up to any of the Tremaynes.

"Bullet come nigh me just now. Better I tend to business for a mite."

Boone edged over a little and peered through the chinks in the rocks but could see only the dark line of the forest. The man he had kept under the rock shelf was off to his right now and it was not an easy shot . . . anyway, he had suffered enough.

His mouth felt dry and he rinsed it carefully with water from his canteen, then let the cool water trickle down his parched throat. It was his first drink in many hours. His face felt hot and there was a queer feeling around the wound in his side.

Bullets snarled and snapped, biting at the rocks, near him and further along. He held his fire, reluctant to give himself away. Boone found no malice in his heart for the officers of the law. This was their job, and not theirs to decide the right and wrong, but to bring him in. He moved, crawling back along the long undercut of the cave. There was a little more to write. Ten . . . maybe twenty minutes more. Then it could be over . . . he could finally let it be over.

"Ebberly, Son, he made his brags, but we kept away from him. Only we shouldn't have. He knowed we was in town and when we kept away he figured we was scared. Then he seen Burt and took a shot at him. Burt shot back. Both of them missed.

"Burt, he hunted him and lost him. It was me who run into Ebberly last. I come down the street afore noon, hunting a couple of copper rivets to use in fixing my saddle. He stepped down into the street and yells at me, 'Boone Tremayne!'

"He yelled, and he shot. Yet my gun come up so fast the two shots sounded like one. Only he missed . . . I didn't. I stood there, looking around. 'Folks,' I said, 'I'm surely Boone Tremayne. But none of us, my brothers or me, ever stole a thing off any man. Nor we never shot at no man unless he hunted us down. We got us a bad name, but it ain't our doing. You seen this . . . he come at me with a drawn gun.'

" 'You all better ride,' a feller says. 'This here Seth Bullock, our sheriff, he'd have to take you in.' So we rode out. Sam was kilt and Ma was dead and everywhere they was after us.

"We headed west, making for the Hole-in-the-Wall where men beyond the law would be let alone. We come down Beaver Crick out of the Black Hills and we rode up Cemetery Ridge and we drawed up there and rested our horses.

"After awhile Lisha, he tunes up his old gitar and starts to play a might, and then we saw a feller coming up the slope. He looked a mighty rough customer and when he heerd our music he slowed up and looked us over. Then he come on up clost.

" 'Howdy!' he says. 'Goin' far?'

" 'To Sundance,' Burt says, 'How fer is it?'

" 'Mebbe fifteen mile,' this gent says. 'Luck!' An' he rides on.

" 'Didn't like the look o' that hombre,' Burt says, 'we better ride out o' here, an' not for Sundance!' So we mounted up and took out south, holding east of Bald Mountain right along the Wyoming–South Dakota line.

"Sure enough, Son, that gent was no good. He headed hisself right for Sundance, warning folks at ranches as he rode. The Bloody Tremaynes was riding he said. We seen the first posse when we was heading to Lost Canyon, but there was no fight until they closed in on us from three directions at Stockade Beaver Crick. We fought her out there, kilt four of them and scratched up a few more, but we lost Burt. He had three bullets in him when he went down, kilt two men before he died. We buried Burt there on Stockade Beaver, and we made a marker for him, which you'll see if you ever ride thataway.

"We rode south and west with that there posse setting in the brush licking their wounds.

"We made the Hole-in-the-Wall and rode through and no posse would foller us. We'd no money, only the horses we rode. But we run into a short-handed cow outfit driving to the Buffalo Fork. They didn't know who we was and didn't give two boots in a rain barrel. We done our share like always, and we stuck to our ownselves. The hands, they was friendly cusses, and the boss he only asked from a man a day's work. We drove to the Buffalo Fork and then the boss, he come over to us. 'I'll be payin' you off in the mornin'. You boys better buy what ca'tridges we got,' he says, quiet-like, 'you won't find no place clost by to git 'em.'

" 'That's right friendly o' you, Boss,' Lisha says, 'we take it kindly.'

"He stands there a mite, and then he says, 'Never did b'lieve all I heerd, anyways,' he said, and then he smiled. 'We'll sure miss that music you boys make. Would you strike us up some singin' afore you leave?'

"So we done it. Lisha, he sung *Greensleeves,* and *Brennan on the Moor,* an' *On Top of Ol' Smoky* and some of the other old songs from the hills back yonder, songs our folks fetched from Scotland and Ireland. We sang for an evening, and then loaded up with grub and bullets, and took off. Southwest across the Blackrock and camped at Lily Lake, and then on to the Gross Venture and into the Jackson Hole country.

"Son, your Pa's hands is mighty cold now. I guess this here letter's got to end up.

"Johnny, he wanted to see Ellie Winters, and Lisha, he wanted to eat fresh melons from the patch, and I wanted to see your Ma again. I never knowed she loved me. I never even guessed she cared or thought of me. I just figured I'd like to see her some.

"One night we was setting by the fire and Lisha he looked over at me and he says, 'Boys, the melons'll be ripe in the bottom land now, an' the horses will be headin' up from the flats for the high meadows.' So then we knowed we was heading home.

"We rode down the Snake to the Grey and down the Grey to the Bear, and we followed her south to the border, staying clear of ranches and towns. Of a night we built our fires small and covered them well, and then at last we come riding down to the hills near Durango.

"Lisha, he chuckles and says to me, 'You all sure been a-talkin' a lot in your sleep, boy. If'n you ever said those things to a girl awake she'd sure be bakin' your corn pone from here on out.'

"Me, I git all redded up. 'Don't give me that,' I say, 'I never talked none. Anyway, it wouldn't matter. What woman would care for me?'

"Both Lisha and Johnny looked up sharp. 'You damn fool!' they says, 'they'd never git a better man, nowheres. An' that Marge, she's been eatin' her heart out for years over you!'

"Me, I just stood there . . . I never figured nothing like that. I sure thought they was wrong, but both them boys, they knowed a sight more about women than ever I would.

"Lisha, he rides off to town, and he ain't gone an hour afore he comes back and then Ellie, she and Marge comes a-running, and with them is Betts Warner, Lisha's girl. Marge, she just stopped, took one look, and then run to me and went to crying in my arms.

"We made her a triple weddin' just two days later, but folks heerd about it, and one morning Lisha come to the door for his horse and Dick Watson, his brother and four-five friends, they shot him down. Shot him down with him only getting one shot off.

"Betts, she come a-running to warn us, thinking of us even when her heart was gone within her, her man laying dead back there full of Watson lead.

" 'Saddle up,' I says to Johnny, 'I'll be coming back soon.' Me, I buckled on my guns.

" 'I'm goin' with you,' Johnny says, and I told him no. He'd have to git us packed and ready. Marge, she just looked at me strange and soft and proud. She says, 'You go along, Boone, I'll saddle up for you, and I'll be a-waiting here when you get back.'

"Never a mite of complaining, never a word again it. She was a man's woman, that one, and she knowed my way was to ride for the man who fetched this trouble down upon us.

"It was bright noonday when I fetched up to town. I swung down from the saddle and I asked old Jake. 'You go along,' I said, 'and you tell that Dick Watson I'm here to put him down.'

"Standin' there, I wondered if it was I'd never have me a home, or see the light in my baby's eyes, or see the sunlight on the green corn growing, or smell the hay from my own meadows. Them things was all I ever wanted, all I ever fixed to have, and now it seemed like all my life I toted a gun, shooting and being shot at.

"All I ever wanted in this here world was a bit of land and peace, the way man was meant to live. Not with no gun in his hand a-killing folks.

"I seen Dick Watson step from a door down the way, I seen him start, and I pulled down my hat and stepped out, stepped out and started walking to kill a man.

"Then Watson stopped and I looked across the forty paces at him and I made my voice strong in the street. 'Dick Watson, you brung hell to my family. You was sore because that black mare beat your horse! You lied about us stealing! You made us into outlaws and caused my brothers to be kilt and some other men too. It'll be on your conscience whether you live or die.'

"He stood there staring at me like he'd looked right in the face of death, and then he slapped leather. His gun came up and I shot him, low down in the belly where they die slow and hard. God forgive me, but I done it with hate in my heart. And then . . . I should have knowed he'd framed it, a half dozen of his friends stepped out and opened up on me.

"Son, what come over me then I don't

know. I guess I went sort of crazy. When I seen them all around me, I just tore loose and went to shooting. I went up on the porch after them, I followed one up the stairs and into his room. I chased another and shot him running, and then I loaded up and turned my back on both the dead and the living and I walked down that street to my horse. I was halfway home before I knowed I'd a bullet in me.

"When I was patched up some we rode on and Betts went back to her folks, a widow almost afore she was a wife. We fetched up, final, in the Blue Mountains of Utah, and there we built us a double cabin and we ketched wild horses and hunted desert honey, just the two boys of us left from the five we'd been. We lived there and for months we was happy.

"Your Ma was the finest ever, Son. I never knowed what it could be like to live with no woman, nor to have her there, always knowing how I felt inside when nobody had ever knowed before. We walked together and talked together and day by day the running and shooting seemed farther and farther away.

"Johnny was happy, too. Them days his mouth organ laughed and cried and sang sweet songs to the low moon and the high sun, and he played the corn out of the ground and the good sweet melons. We hunted some and we lived quiet-like and happy. How long? Three months, five months . . . and then Marge comes to me and says Ellie's got to go where she can have a doc. She's to have a baby and something, she's sure, ain't right about it.

"We knowed what it meant, but life must go on, Son, and you were to be born and I aimed to give you what start I could. The same for Johnny. So we gathered our horses and we rode out to Salt Lake with the girls. We sold our horses for cash money to some Mormons, and then we drifted north. The girls had to stay with the Doc awhile, so we got us a riding job each.

"One day a gent comes into a bar where we was with a star on him and he sees me setting by the window. Marge's time is coming nigh and we're all a-waiting like. This man with the star he comes over and drops into a chair near Johnny and me. 'Mighty hot day!' he says. 'Too hot to hunt outlaws, especially,' he says, 'when they size up like good, God-fearin' folks.

" 'I got me a paper says them Tremaynes is hereabouts. I'm to hunt 'em up an' arrest 'em, what do you boys think about that?'

" 'We reckon,' Johnny says, very quiet, 'them Tremaynes never bothered nobody if they was let alone.'

"He nods his head. 'I heard that, too,' he says, 'Leastways, if they've been in town they sure been mighty quiet an' well-behaved folks. Worst of it is,' he got up, wiping the sweat-band of his hat, 'I took an oath to do my duty. Now, the way I figure that doesn't mean I have to go r'arin' out in the heat of the day. But come sundown,' he spoke slow and careful, 'I'm gonna hunt them Tremaynes up.'

"That sheriff, Son, he looked up at Johnny and then over at me. 'I got two sons,' he said quietly, 'and if the Tremaynes left family in this town, they'd be protected as long as me and my sons lived.'

"We didn't take long about saying goodbye, although we never knowed it was our last. We never guessed we was riding out of town and right to our death.

"It was fifty miles east that we passed a gent on the trail. We never knowed him but he turned an' looked after us. And that done, he hightailed it to the nearest town and before day a posse was in the saddle.

"At noon, from a high ridge, we drawed up and looked back. We seen four separate dust clouds. Johnny, he looked at me and grinned. 'I reckon we ain't in no hurry no more,' he said, 'they got us again' the mountains.' He looked up at them twelve, and thirteen thousand foot peaks. 'I wonder if any man ever went through up there?'

" 'We can give her a try,' I said quiet. 'Not much else we can do.'

" 'Horses are shot, Boone,' he replies, 'I ain't goin' to kill no good horse for those lousy coyotes back yonder.' So we got down and walked, our saddle-bags loose and rifles in our hands.

"Then we heard them on the trail behind and we drawed off and slipped our saddles from the horses and cached them in the brush. Cow Hollow, Son, and that's where we made our stand. We had a plenty of ammunition, and we weren't wasteful, making shots count. We hunkered down among the rocks and trees and stood them off.

"Morning left us and the noon, and the high hot sun bloomed in the sky, but it was late fall, and as the afternoon drew on, a cold wind began to blow.

"They come then, they come like Injuns through the woods after us, and we opened up, and then suddenly Johnny was on his feet, he's got that old Winchester at his hip and he shoots and then he jumps right into them clubbing with his rifle. He went down, and I went over the rocks, both guns going, and that bunch broke and ran.

"I fetched Johnny back, and he lay there looking up at me. 'Good old Boone!' he said. 'Get the girls and get away. Go to Mexico, go somewheres, but get away!'

"He died like that, and I sat right there and cried. Then I covered him over gentle and I slipped out of Cow Hollow and started up the trail toward the high peaks.

"It was cold, mighty cold. The sun came up and touched those white peaks and ridges ahead of me, then the clouds covered her over and it began to snow. I walked on, and the snow stopped but the wind blew colder and colder. We was getting high up, I passed the timber-line here on Tokewanna and crawled into this here place.

"Son, I can't see to write no more, and there ain't no more to say. I guess I didn't say it well, but there she is. You can read her and make up your own mind. This here I've addressed to your mother, care of that sheriff down there. I even got a stamp to put on so's it will be U.S. mail and no one'll dare open her up.

"Be a good boy, Son, love your Ma and do like she tells you. And carry the name of Tremayne with pride. It was honest blood, no matter what you hear from anyone."

He was stiff from the cold, but he rolled over carefully and folded the letter and tucked it into an envelope. On it he placed his stamp, and then scrawled the name of his wife, in care of the sheriff. From his throat he took a black handkerchief and fastened it to a stick so its flapping would draw attention. Near it, held down by a rock, he left the letter.

Then he crawled out and using his rifle as a crutch, got to his feet. He still had ammunition. He had no food. He discarded the almost empty canteen. For a long time he looked down the cold flank of the mountain into the dark fringe of trees. Far away among those trees flickered the ghostlike fingers of fire, where men warmed themselves and talked, or slept.

Something blurred his eyes. His head

throbbed. Pain gnawed at his side and his leg was stiff. How long he stood there he did not know; swaying gently, not quite delirious and yet not quite rational. Then he turned slowly and looked up, two thousand feet, to the cold and icy peak, silver and magnificent in its solemn grandeur.

He stared for a long time, and then he began to climb. It was very slow, it was very hard. He pulled his old hat down, put the scarf lower around his ears. To the left there was a ridge, and beyond the ridge there would be a valley.

He climbed and then he slipped, lacerating his hands on the icy rocks. He got up, pushing himself on.

"Marge," he whispered, "Son . . ." He continued to move. Crawling . . . falling . . . standing . . . he felt the snow, felt his feet sink. He seemed to have enormously large feet, enormously heavy. "Never aimed to kill nobody," he said. He climbed on . . . wind stirred the icy bits of snow over the harsh flank of the mountain. He bowed his head, and when he turned his face from the wind he looked down and saw the fires below like tiny stars. How far he had come! How very far!

He turned, and looked up. There was the ridge, not far, not too far . . . and what was it he had thought just a moment ago? Beyond the ridge, there is always a valley.

THE MOON OF THE TREES BROKEN BY SNOW

Cold blew the winds along the canyon, moaning in the cedars, whining softly where the sagebrush grew. Their fire was small, and they huddled close, the firelight playing shadow games on the walls, the walls their grandfather's father built when he moved from the pit house atop the mesa to the great arch of the shallow cave.

"We must go," the boy said, "there is no more wood for burning, and the strength is gone from the earth. Our crops are thin, and when the snows have gone, the wild ones will come again, and they will kill us."

"It is so," his mother agreed. "One by one the others have left, and we are not enough to keep open the ditches that water our fields, nor defend against the wild ones."

"Where will we go?" Small Sister asked.

They avoided looking at each other, their eyes hollow with fear, for they knew not where to go. Drought lay heavy upon the land, and from north, south, east, and west others had come seeking, no place seeming better than another. Was it not better to die here, where they had lived?

The boy was gaunt for each day he hunted farther afield and each day found less to hunt. Small Sister and his mother gathered brush or looted timbers from abandoned dwellings to keep their fires alight.

The Old One stirred and mumbled. "In my sleep I saw them," he muttered, "strange men sitting upon strange beasts."

"He is old," their mother said. "His thoughts wander."

How old he was they did not know. He had come out of the desert and they cared for him. None knew what manner of man he was, but it was said he talked to gods, and they with him.

"Strange men," he said, "with robes that glisten."

"How many men?" The boy asked without curiosity but because he knew that to live, an old one must be listened to and questioned sometimes.

"Three," the Old One said, "no more."

Firelight flickered on the parchment of his ancient face. "Sitting upon beasts," he repeated.

Sitting upon? What manner of beast? And why sit upon them? The boy went to a corner for an old timber. A hundred years ago it had been a tree; then part of a roof; now it was fuel.

They must leave or die, and it was better to die while doing than sitting. There was no corn left in the storage place. Even the rats were gone.

"When the light comes," the boy said, "we will go."

"What of the Old One? His limbs are weak."

"So are we all," the boy said. "Let him walk as far as he may."

"They followed the path," the Old One said, "a path where there was no path. They went where the light was."

On the third day their water was gone, but the boy knew of a seep. At the foot of the rocks he dug into the sand. When the sand grew damp, they held it against their brows, liking its coolness. Water seeped into the hollow, and one by one they drank.

They ate of the corn they carried, but some they must not eat. It would be seed for planting in the new place—if they found it.

During the night snow fell. They filled a water sack made of skin and started on.

With the morning the snow vanished. Here and there a few seeds still clung to the brush. Under an ironwood they rested, picking seed from the ground. They could be parched and eaten or ground into pinole. As they walked they did not cease from looking, and the Old One found many seeds, although his eyes were bad.

"Where do we go?" Small Sister asked.

"We go," the boy replied, but inside he felt cold shivers as when one eats too much of the prickly-pear fruit. He did not know where they went, and he was much afraid.

On the ninth day they ate the last of their corn but for that which must be kept for seed. Twice the boy snared ground squirrels, and three times he killed lizards. One day they stopped at a spring, gathering roots of a kind of wild potato that the people to the south called *iikof*. His mother and the Old One dug them from the flat below the spring.

Day after day they plodded onward, and the cold grew. It snowed again, and this time it did not go away. The Old One lagged farther and farther behind, and each day it took him longer to reach the fire.

The boy did not meet their eyes now, for they looked to him, and he had nothing to promise.

"There was a path of light," the Old One muttered. "They followed the path."

He drew his worn blanket about his thin shoulders. "It is the Moon of the Limbs of Trees Broken by Snow," he whispered, "that was the time."

"What time, Old One?" The boy tried to be patient.

"The time of the path. They followed the path."

"We have seen no path, Old One."

"The path was light. No man had walked where the path lay."

"Why, then, did they follow? Were they fools?"

"They followed the path because they heard and they believed."

"Heard what? Believed in what?"

"I do not know. It came while I slept. I do not know what they believed, only that they believed."

"I believe we are lost," Small Sister said.

The mother looked to the boy. He was the man, although but a small man, and alone. "In the morning we will go on," he said.

The Old One arose. "Come," he said. Wondering, the boy followed.

Out in the night they went, stopping where no firelight was. The Old One lifted his staff. "There!" he said. "There lies the path!"

"I see no path," the boy said, "only a star."

"The star is the path," the Old One said, "if you believe."

It was a bright star, hanging in the southern sky. The boy looked at it, and his lips trembled. He had but twelve summers. Yet he was the man, and he was afraid.

"The star is the path," the Old One said.

"How can one believe in a star?" the boy protested.

"You do not have to believe in the star. They traveled for a reason. We travel for another. But you can believe in yourself, believe in the good you would do. The men of the star were long ago and not like us. It was only a dream."

The Old One went back to the fire and left the boy alone. They trusted him, and he did not trust himself. They had faith, and he had none. He led them into a wilderness—to what?

He had wandered, hoping. He had found nothing. He had longed, but the longing was empty. He found no place for planting, no food nor fuel.

He looked again. Was not that one star brighter than all the rest? Or did he only believe it so?

The Old One had said, "They followed a star."

He looked at the star. Then stepping back of a tall spear of yucca, he looked across it at the star. Then breaking off another spear, he set it in the sand and lined it up on the star so he would know the direction of the star when dawn came.

To lead them, he must believe. He would believe in the star.

When morning came, they took up their packs. Only the Old One sat withdrawn, unmoving. "It is enough," he said. "I can go no further."

"You will come. You taught me to have faith; you, too, must have it."

Day followed day, and night followed night. Each night the boy lined up his star with a peak, a tree, or a rock. On three of the days they had no food, and two days were without water. They broke the spines from cactus and sucked on the pulp from the thick leaves.

Small Sister's feet were swollen and the

flesh broken. "It is enough," his mother said. "We can go no further."

They had come to a place where cottonwoods grew. He dug a hole in the streambed and found a little water. They soaked cottonwood leaves and bound them to Small Sister's feet. "In the morning," he said, "we will go on."

"I cannot," Small Sister said.

With dead branches from the cottonwoods he built a fire. They broiled the flesh of a terrapin found on the desert. Little though there was, they shared it.

The boy walked out in the darkness alone. He looked up and the star was there. "All right," he said.

When the light came, he shouldered his pack, and they looked at him. He turned to go, and one by one they followed. The Old One was the last to rise.

Now the land was broken by canyons. There was more cedar, occasionally a piñon. It snowed in the night, and the ground was covered, so they found only those seeds that still hung in their dry pods. They were very few.

Often they waited for the Old One. The walking was harder now, and the boy's heart grew small within him. At last they stopped to rest, and his mother looked at him: "It is no use. I cannot go on."

Small Sister said nothing and the Old One took a long time coming to where they waited.

"Do you stay then?" the boy said. "I will go on."

"If you do not come back?"

"Then you are better without me," he said. "If I can, I will come."

Out of their sight he sat down and put his head in his hands. He had failed them. The Old One's medicine had failed. Yet he knew he must try. Small though he was, he was the man. He walked on, his thoughts no longer clear. Once he fell, and again he caught himself on a rock before falling. He straightened, blinking to clear his vision.

On the sand before him was a track, the track of a deer. He walked on and saw other tracks, those of a raccoon, and the raccoon liked water. Not in two months had he seen the track of an animal. They led away down the canyon.

He went out on the rocks and caught himself abruptly, almost falling over the rim. It was a limestone sink, and it was filled with water. He took up a stone and dropped it, and it hit the pool and sank with a deep, rich, satisfying sound. The well was deep and wide, with a stream running from one side.

He went around the rim and lay down flat to drink of the stream. Something stirred near him, and he looked up quickly.

They were there: his mother, Small Sister, and the Old One. He stood up, very straight, and he said, "This is our place; we will stop here."

The boy killed a deer, and they ate. He wiped his fingers on his buckskin leggings and said, "Those who sat upon the beasts? What did they find, following their star?"

"A cave that smelled of animals where a baby lay on dry grass. The baby's father and mother were there, and some other men wearing skins, who stood by with bowed heads."

"And the shining ones who sat upon the beasts?"

"They knelt before the baby and offered it gifts."

"It is a strange story," the boy said, "and at another time I will listen to it again. Now we must think of planting."

MORAN OF THE TIGERS

Flash Moran took the ball on the Rangers' thirty yard line, running with his head up, eyes alert. He was a money player, and a ground gainer who took the openings where he found them.

The play was called for off tackle. Murphy had the hole open for him, and Flash put his head down and went through, running like a madman. He hit a two-hundred-pound tackle in the midriff and set him back ten feet and plowed on for nine yards before he was downed.

Higgins called for a pass and Flash

dropped back and took the ball. Swindler went around end fast and was cutting over when Flash rifled the ball to him with a pass that fairly smoked. He took it without slowing and started for the end zone. Weaving, a big Ranger lineman missed him, and he went on to be downed on the two yard line by a Ranger named Fenton, a wiry lad new in pro football.

"All right, Flash," Higgins said as they trotted back. "I'm sending you right through the middle for this one."

Flash nodded. The ball was snapped, and as Higgins wheeled and shoved it into his middle, he turned sharply and went through the line with a crash of leather that could be heard in the top rows. He went through and he was downed safely in the end zone. He got up as the whistle shrilled, and grinned at Higgins. "Well, there's another one for Pop. If we can keep this up, the Old Man will be in the money again."

"Right." Tom Higgins was limping a little, but grinning. "It's lucky for him he's got a loyal bunch. Not a man offered to back out when he laid his cards on the table."

"No," Flash agreed, "but I'm worried. Lon Cramp has been after some of the boys. He's got money, and he's willing to pay anything to get in there with a championship team. He's already got Johnny Hill from the Rangers, doubled his salary, and he got Kowalski from the Brewers. He hasn't started on us, but I'm expecting it."

"It'll be you he's after," Tom Higgins said, glancing at the big halfback. "You were the biggest ground gainer in the league last year, and a triple-threat man."

"Maybe. But there's others, too. Hagan, for instance. And he needs the money with all those operations for his wife. He's the best tackle in pro football."

•   •   •

Pop Dolan was standing in the dressing room grinning when they came in. "Thanks, boys," he said, "I can't tell you what this means to me. I don't mean the winning, so much as the loyalty."

Flash Moran sat down and began to unlace his shoes. Pop Dolan had started in pro football on a shoestring and a lot of goodwill. He had made it pay. His first two years had been successful beyond anybody's expectations, but Pop hadn't banked all the money, he had split a good third of the take with the team, over and above their salaries. "You earned it," he said simply. "When I make money, we all make it."

Well, Flash thought, he's losing now, and if we take the winnings we've got to take the punishment. Yet how many of the players felt that way? Tom Higgins, yes. Dolan had discovered Tom in the mines of Colorado. He had coached him through college, and the two were close as father and son. Hagan?

He didn't know. Butch Hagan was the mainstay of the big line. An intercollegiate heavyweight wrestling champ, he had drive and power to spare. Ken Martin? The handsome Tiger tailback, famous college star and glamour boy of pro football, was another doubtful one. He was practically engaged to "Micky" Dolan, Pop's flame-haired daughter, so that would probably keep him in line.

Flash dressed and walked outside, then turned and strolled away toward the line of cabs that stood waiting.

A slender, sallow-faced man was standing by a black car as he approached, and he looked up at Flash, smiling. "Hi, Moran!" He thrust out a cold limp hand. "Want a ride uptown?"

Flash looked at him, then shrugged. It wasn't unusual. Lots of sports fans liked to talk to athletes, and the ride would save him the cab fare as his car was in the shop. He got in.

"You live at the Metropole, don't you?"

the stranger asked. "How about dropping by the Parkway for a steak? I want to
talk a little. My name is Rossaro. Jinx
Rossaro."

"A steak? Well, why not?" They rode
on in silence until the car swung into the
drive of the Parkway. It was a twenty-
story apartment hotel, and quite a place.
The kind of place Flash Moran couldn't
afford. He was wondering, now . . . Jinx
Rossaro . . . The name sounded familiar
but he couldn't place it. He shrugged.
Well, what the devil? He wasn't any high-
school girl who had to be careful about
pickups.

The dining room was spotless and the
hush that prevailed was broken only by
the tinkle of glass and silver. Somewhere,
beyond the range of his eyes, an orchestra
played a waltz by Strauss. They did things
well here, he reflected. This Rossaro—

Another man was approaching their
table. A short, square man who looked all
soft and silky, until you saw his eyes.

Then he looked hard. He walked up and held out his hand. "How are you, Jinx? And this is the great Flash Moran?"

There was no sarcasm in the man. His hard little eyes spanned Moran's shoulders and took in his lean, hard two hundred pounds. "I'm happy to meet you. My name is Cramp, Lon Cramp."

Flash had risen to acknowledge the introduction. His eyes narrowed a little as they often did when he saw an opposing tackler start toward him.

They sat down and he looked across at Cramp. "If the occasion is purely social, Mr. Cramp, I'm going to enjoy it. If you got me here to offer me a job, I'm not interested."

Cramp smiled. "How much money do you make, Mr. Moran?"

"You probably know as well as I do. I'm getting fifteen thousand for the season."

"If you get paid. To pay you Dolan must make money. He's broke now, and he won't win any more games. I think,

Moran, you'd better listen to what I have to say."

"I wouldn't think of leaving Pop," Flash said quietly. "I'm not a college boy. I came off a cow ranch to the Marines. After the Marines, where I played some football in training, Pop found me and gave me all the real coaching I had, so I owe a lot to him."

"Of course," Cramp smiled, then he leaned forward, "but you owe something to yourself, too. You haven't long, no man has, in professional football. You have to get what you can when you can get it. Pop's through. We know that, and you must realize it yourself. You can't help him."

"I'm not a rat. If the ship sinks I'll go down with it."

"Very noble. But impractical. And," Cramp leaned forward again, "it isn't as if you would have to leave Dolan."

Flash straightened. "Just what do you mean?"

"My friend, we are businessmen. I want the professional championship. You would be infinitely more valuable on Dolan's team than on mine—if you were on my payroll, too."

"You mean—?" Flash's face was tight, his eyes hard.

"That you play badly? Certainly not! You play your best game, until, shall we say, the critical moment. Then, perhaps a fumble, a bad kick—you understand?" Cramp smiled smoothly.

Flash pushed back his chair, then he leaned forward. "I understand very well. You're not a sportsman, you're a crook! I not only won't do your dirty work, but I'll see nobody else does!"

Cramp's eyes were deadly. "Those were hard words, Moran. Reconsider when your temper cools, and my offer stands. For two days only. Then—watch yourself!"

Moran wheeled and walked out. He

was mad, and mad clear through, yet underneath his anger there was a cool, hardheaded reasoning that told him this was something Dolan couldn't buck. Dolan was honest. Cramp had the money to spend . . . if Flash wouldn't cooperate, there were others.

There was Hagan, who needed money. Hagan who could fail to open a hole, who could let a tackler by him, who could run too slowly and block out one of his own players. Would Butch do it? Flash shook his head. He wouldn't—usually. Now his wife was ill and he was broke as they all were. . . .

Higgins? He would stand by. Most of the others would, too. Flash walked back to his room, and lay down on the bed. He did not even open his eyes when Higgins came in, undressed, and turned in.

•   •   •

Dolan met him in the coffee shop for breakfast. He looked bad, dark circles under his eyes, and he showed lack of sleep. Tom Higgins was with him, so was Ken Martin. Ken, looking tall and bronzed and strong, beside him, Micky.

Flash felt a sharp pang. He was in love with Micky Dolan. He had never deceived himself about that. Yet it was always the handsome Martin who was with her, always the sharp-looking former All-American.

"Well, it's happened!" Pop said suddenly. "Cramp raided me yesterday. He got Wilson and Krakoff."

Moran felt himself go sick. Krakoff was their big center. He had been with the team for three years. None of them were working under contract this year, not in the strictest sense. Pop leaned over backwards in being fair. Any agreement could be terminated if the player wished. Krakoff at twenty-two was a power in the line. Wilson had been a substitute back, but a good one. They had been short-handed before this happened.

Martin looked at Flash thoughtfully. "Didn't I see you going off the field with Rossaro?"

Moran looked up and said quietly. "Rossaro met me with an offer to drive me home. When we got up to dinner, Cramp was there. He made me an offer."

Micky was looking at him, her eyes very steady. "I told him nothing doing."

Ken Martin was still staring at him. So was Micky, but neither of them said a word.

It wasn't until they met the Shippers on Friday that the extent of the damage was visible. The Shippers were big and rough. Dolan's Tigers had beaten them a month before in a hard-fought game, but hadn't beaten them decisively. Now it was different.

Jalkan, the big Shipper fullback, carried

the ball through the middle on the first play. He went right through where Krakoff had stopped him cold a month before. He went for five yards then Higgins nailed him.

They lined up, and Jalkan came right through again for four yards. Then on a fake, Duffy got away for fourteen, and the Shippers really began to march. They rolled down the field and nothing the Tigers could do would stop them. Duffy got away again and made twenty yards around end before Moran angled downfield and hit him hard on the eight yard line.

But it was only a momentary setback, for Jalkan came through the middle again, nearly wrecking Burgess, a husky Tiger guard, in the process. He was downed by Martin on the two yard line, but went over on the next play.

Then they repeated. Duffy got in the clear and took a pass from Jalkan and made twenty yards before he was doomed by Martin. The Tigers lined up and began to battle, but they weren't clicking. Even Flash, fighting with everything he had, could see that. Krakoff had left a big hole at center, a hole that Worth, the substitute, could never begin to fill. Burgess, the right guard, was badly hurt. They were working him, deliberately, it seemed to Moran. The center of the line was awfully soft.

At the half, the score was twenty to nothing, and the team trooped into the dressing room, tired and battered. Burgess had taken a fearful beating. Dolan looked at him, and shook his head. "No use you going out there again, Bud," he said. "We'll let Noble go in."

Ken Martin looked up, and then his eyes shifted to Flash. They all knew what that meant. Noble was big and strong, but he was slower than Burgess. That hole at center was going to be awfully weak.

"We'll be taking the kick," Dolan said simply, "let's get that ball and get on down the field."

Moran took the kick and started down the field. Every yard counted now, and he was making time. He was crossing their own forty yard line when Jalkan cut in toward him. He cross-stepped quickly, in an effort to get away, and smacked into a heavy shoulder. Thrown off balance he was knocked squarely into Jalkan's path and the big Shipper hit him like a pile-driver with a thud they could hear high in the stands.

Rolling over and over, Flash was suddenly stopped when the pile-up came. He got slowly to his feet, badly shaken. Martin stared at him. "What did you run into me for? You could have gotten away from Jalkan!"

"What?" Puzzled, he stared at Martin. Then he noticed Butch Hagan looking at him queerly. Frowning, he trotted back into position. Higgins called for twenty-two, and that meant Flash was to go around the end for a pass, and he went fast. He got down the field, saw Ken drop back with the ball, and then it came whistling over!

He glanced over his shoulder and saw with wild panic that he was never going to make it. It was leading him too much. Hurling every ounce of speed he had, he threw himself at the ball, missed, it hit the ground and was recovered by the Shipper tailback.

Schaumberg, the rangy Tiger end, glanced at him. "What's the matter?" he asked sharply. "Cramp got to you, too?"

His answer froze on his lips. Hot words would do no good at this time. He started to reply, but Schaumberg was trotting away. His head down, Flash rounded into position. He noticed Higgins glance at him, and Ken Martin was smiling cynically.

• • •

The Tigers kept trying. They made two first downs through the big Shipper wall with Ken Martin's twelve-yard reverse sparking the drive. Then a Shipper end spilled through and squelched a spinner, and the Tigers had to kick.

Higgins toed the ball into the corner, and it didn't bounce out.

Duffy fell back as if for a kick, but the Shipper's Jalkan took the ball and powered it through for five yards. They continued to feed him the pigskin for three downs, and he ran the ball back out of danger.

Then Duffy got loose. The flashy Irishman got into the secondary, and he was running like Red Grange. When Flash drove for him he met a stiffarm that dropped him in his tracks. Duffy was away and going fast. He was a wizard on his feet, anyway, and today he was running as if possessed.

Ken Martin cut down the field heading for him, but Duffy had a hidden burst of speed, and he pulled the trigger on it and cut back across the field, Martin swerved, lost distance, gained, and then made a dive that left his arms empty and Duffy went across the goal line standing up.

It was sheer murder. Duffy was playing way over his head, and Jalkan seemed to have more drive than normal. Against the weakened Tiger line even less worthy opponents would have had a field day; as it was, Jalkan pulverized them, and Duffy kept the backfield in a dither.

Then, with four minutes to go, Flash got away and Martin dropped back for a pass. The ball came over like a bullet, and Flash glimpsed it, then let his legs out. He was in an open field and there wasn't a man between him and the goal posts. The ball was leading him, he ran like a mad-man, stretched and got his fingertips on it, almost had it, then it eeled from his fingers and dropped, hitting the ground. Pounding feet warned him, and with a frantic dive he made a recovery.

When the pile untangled he got up slowly. Schaumberg stared at him, but said nothing. Makin, a Shipper end, stood looking at him and then said, "We don't need any help. We can win it without you."

Flash froze. Then he wheeled and started for Makin. Somebody yelled, and Makin said, "All right, come an' get it!" He threw a right. Flash slipped it, and smashed him in the ribs with his own. A left caught him over the eye, but it bounced off the padding of his helmet, and then he was jerked back and the referee was yelling at him. "Cut it out or get off the field!"

Without a word he pulled himself free and walked back. Tom Higgins took the ball and went through tackle for three, then Martin for two, and then Higgins took it over for their only score of the game.

Slowly, Flash started for the dressing rooms. Higgins was limping. As if it hadn't been enough to lose Wilson and Krakoff, now Burgess and Higgins were both hurt. He started toward Schaumberg, but the big German deliberately walked away from him, and Moran stopped.

Pop Dolan was standing by the door with Micky. His face was pale. Ken Martin was talking to him, then Martin shrugged and walked into the dressing room. Flash stopped.

Micky looked at him, her eyes scornful. "Well," she said, "you probably earned *your* money!"

Moran felt himself turn sick inside. He turned to her, "What makes you say that?" he demanded. "I do my best!"

"Do you?" she inquired. "But for whom? Dad, or Lon Cramp?"

Moran stared at them, pale and helpless.

Even Pop suspected him. "What are you thinking of me?" he burst out. "Men have missed taking passes before!"

"After talking with Cramp?" Micky demanded. "And you, Moran, you who were supposed to be so grateful! You, who never missed a pass!"

For a moment, he stared at them, and then he turned and walked inside. There was dead silence when he came in, and he walked across to his locker and began to strip. He didn't even bother to shower, just dressed, and no one spoke, no one said a word.

Micky and Pop had gone when he got outside. He walked slowly across the street and got into his car. Rossaro was leaning against it, waiting for him. "See how it goes when you don't play ball?" The smaller man arched an eyebrow and sauntered off and Flash watched him go.

Just what, he asked himself suddenly,

had Rossaro meant by that? Those passes. . . . But that would mean that Ken Martin was taking a payoff from Cramp. And Ken was going to marry Micky Dolan. It didn't make sense. Even from a selfish standpoint, it would be much better to marry Micky if Pop owned a successful club.

On the inspiration of a moment, he swung his coupe into a side street and turned it to face the highway. Who had Rossaro been waiting for?

He had only to wait a minute. Rossaro came by in the big black car, and there were two men in the backseat with him. Who they were he couldn't make out. He waited what seemed a full minute, then swung out and began to follow them. Up the drive and down the street toward the Parkway. Suddenly they turned sharp left and went down a street that led toward the country. He fell back a little further, puzzled, but alert.

The black car swung off the highway

and took to the woods. He waited an instant, then followed. Ahead of him, the car was stopped. Hastily, he swung his own car into a side road and got out.

He was almost up to the black car when he heard a slight noise. He moved forward, through the brush, and then he saw Rossaro. The Italian was turning, then recognition caused a sneer to curl his lips. "Well, Moran! I guess you asked for it. Take him boys!"

Flash tried to turn, then something slugged him, and he staggered. In staggering, he turned. The man he was facing was Makin. Something slammed over his head with terrific force and he fell, tumbling away into an awful, cushiony blackness that smelled strangely of damp earth and pine needles.

When he opened his eyes it was dark. His head was one great throbbing burst of pain. He got his hands under him and pushed up, then lifted to his knees. He could see the dim marks of a dirt road, and then, overhead, the stars. He got shakily to his feet.

It came back, slowly. He had followed Rossaro to see who was with him. They must have guessed who he was, or known, and had turned off and led him into this trap. Makin had been one of them, and they had hit him. When he was facing them, Rossaro must have stepped up and hit him on the head.

He got back to his car. It was there and unharmed. He got in, started the motor, and drove back to his room. When he got to the door, he opened it, staggered in and fell across the bed.

It was daylight when Flash was awakened by the sound of movement. He turned his head and groaned. He heard somebody walking over, and looked up to see Butch Hagan. "What happened to you?" Butch demanded.

Stumblingly, he told him. Hagan stared at him, then got up and dampened a towel. When he came back he went to work on the cut on Moran's head. A long time later, when Flash had bathed and shaved, the two men looked at each other.

"Well," Butch said, "I'll admit, they had me doubting. You always got everything Martin threw and missing two passes, the same way, it didn't look reasonable. Martin swore he put them just as he always had."

"You said 'they' almost convinced you. Who did you mean?"

"Martin and Schaumberg. Both of them said you'd sold out. They said the offer Cramp made you was to fumble or do something to mess up."

Suddenly, Flash looked up. "Butch, I

got an idea that can save the Tigers. Are you with me?"

"Yeah," Hagan said. "I need the dough. I'll admit, I told 'em I'd think it over. But I've got a kid, and—You know how it is, you've got to set an example."

"Yeah." Flash leaned forward. "Butch, did you know Deacon Peabody was working at Denton Mills now?"

"Peabody? Used to be All-American? Why, he was a pal of mine!"

"I know. Now here's what I want you to do. We've got a week until the game with Cramp's Bears. Let's get busy."

Flash came down the stadium steps to the box where Pop Dolan sat with Micky. Pop saw him, and his face got red. Micky saw him too. She started to speak, then tightened her lips and deliberately turned her back on him.

Flash sat down. "Pop," he said, "it's

nearly game time. In a few minutes you'll have a crippled team going out on that field for a beating. You've only got sixteen men down there, and I know for a fact that two of them have sold out."

Pop stared at him, and Micky turned suddenly, her eyes angry, but before she could speak, Flash leaned forward and grabbed Pop Dolan's arm. "Listen, Pop! I know what they told you. But it was all lies! Give me the word and I'll have a winning team on that field when the game starts. They're all here, ready to go!"

"What do you mean?" Pop demanded. "What kind of a team?"

"Pop," Flash said, "you're a square guy. You got friends. Well, I've got them, too. So has Butch Hagan."

Flash stood up and waved, and down on the field near the door to the dressing room, Butch Hagan turned and went through the door. Suddenly, there was a roar, and out on the field came the Bears. They were big, and they were the favorites in today's game, and Flash knew that, even at the odds he had to give, Cramp had bet heavily. The true facts of the Dolan team weren't out, and the fans still believed in them.

There was another roar as the Tigers ran out onto the field. Flash was watching Cramp, and suddenly he saw the gambler stiffen and come erect. There weren't sixteen men out there—there were thirty-five!

Micky sat up suddenly. "Pop, look! That man with the 22 on his jersey! Why, it's Red Saunders!"

"Saunders? But he's not playing football anymore!" Pop said. "He hasn't played since he quit the Tigers two years ago to practice law!"

"And there's Larry Simmons, twice All-American end! And Lew Young, ex-Navy center, and—!"

"We've got you a team!" Flash said. "We've got a team that will win if you give me the word. So what do you say?"

"Why, son," Pop smiled suddenly, "I couldn't make myself believe that you would go back on me!"

"Then we've got a game to play!" Flash said, and slipped away before they could say any more.

He knew it was a good team. Right now there were more stars on that field than there had been in years. Of course, they hadn't all played together, but some of them had. Simmons had played on an Army post team, and Lew Young had played with the Navy, and Saunders had just come back from a hunting trip and was in rare condition. It was a chance, and a good chance.

The Bears had everything in the books. Lon Cramp was out for a title, and he hadn't spared money. He had a big fullback, a ten-second man named Brogan. And the Bears' captain was a lad named

Chadwick who ran like a ghost. Their other backs, both triple-threat men in college ball, were Baykov and Chavel.

The line was bigger than that of the Tigers, and they had power to spare. There was a big tackle named Polanyi, an end with long legs and arms who could run like a streak, and was named Monte Crabb. They had others, too. They had Leland, Barnes, Wilson and, at center, Krakoff.

Red Saunders kicked off for the Tigers and they started down the field. Flash Moran was playing tailback, and he was hanging far back, looking over the team.

Monte Crabb took the ball on the Bear twenty-five yard line and running behind perfect interference got down the field for twenty yards before Larry Simmons cut in, evaded a halfback and dropped Crabb with a bone-jolting tackle.

They lined up and Brogan powered through the center for five yards. Then he took the ball again, and hitting the line, went through for three more before they stopped him.

They drove on until they had rolled the Tigers back to their own ten yard line, but the Tigers were playing good ball. They were getting used to each other, and they were looking over the opposition.

Brogan started through the line, but Butch Hagan shoved Polanyi on his face in the dirt and hit Brogan with everything he had. Brogan clung to the ball, however, and they lined up with a yard lost.

The Tigers held them again, held them without the ball moving an inch, and then on the next play the Tigers' Lew Young and a guard named Corbett hit Krakoff and drove him back on his heels. Krakoff got up mad and took a swing at Young, and Lew, who had been some shakes as an amateur heavyweight, dropped him in his tracks.

They broke that one up, but Krakoff

was mad clear through. He snapped the ball, then drove at Young, and Lew jumped back and Krakoff sprawled forward off balance and Corbett went through that hole and nailed Brogan before he could get out of his tracks. Saunders cut around and as the ball slipped from Brogan's hands, he nailed it and went to the ground.

The Tigers had the ball. Higgins called the signals and Saunders took it around the end for five yards, then they snapped it to Flash and he went off tackle for six. They lined up, and Moran took the ball again, and Red Saunders, running like a deer, got off ahead of him. They went down the sidelines, and he was crossing the Bear forty yard line when he was downed by Chavel.

He was feeling good now, and the team was beginning to click. They liked Pop Dolan, and they didn't like Cramp, and they were out for blood. They weren't saving themselves for another game because most of them weren't expecting to play another.

Flash went around end on the next play and Ken Martin passed. The minute he saw the pass he knew he couldn't make it. He ran like a wild man, but his fingers just grazed the ball. It went down and Chadwick recovered.

Flash turned and started back up the field and saw Schaumberg and Ken Martin standing together. He started toward them, and they stood there waiting for him.

"You deliberately passed that ball out of range!" Flash accused Martin.

"Moran, you're a fool!" Martin said. "If Lon Cramp gets this club you stand to make more money than you ever did!" Suddenly Flash was sure he knew who the other men had been that day in the woods. It had been Makin and Rossario . . . and, in the car, where he could barely be seen, Ken Martin!

"Yeah?" Moran's eyes narrowed. "You seem to know a lot about it!"

"I do," he said harshly. "I'm going to be the manager!"

Unseen by Schaumberg or Martin, Red Saunders had come down behind them and stood listening. Suddenly, he stepped up. "Who's captain of this team?"

"I am," Martin declared flatly. "What about it?"

Red turned abruptly and walked to the edge of the field where he began to talk to Pop. "You get off the field," Flash told Martin. "Captain or not, you're finished!"

"Yeah?" Martin sneered. "You've had this coming for a long time!"

The punch started, but it was a left hook, and too wide. It came up against the padded side of his helmet and Flash let go with an inside right cross that dropped Martin to his haunches. Ken came up fast, and Flash caught him full in the face with one hand then the other! He felt the nose bone crunch under his fist. Then Schaumberg started a punch that was suddenly picked out of the air by Lew Young, who returned it, and Schaumberg went down.

Pop came out on the field then, and his eyes were blazing. The umpire came up, shouting angrily. There were a few words, and Ken Martin and Schaumberg were rushed off the field.

The teams lined up. Brogan tried to come through the center, but Krakoff had taken a beating by then, and when Young hit him he went back on his heels and Higgins went through after Corbett and they dropped Brogan in his tracks.

Flash saw Chadwick catch up a handful of dust and rub it on his palms. It was a habit the swift-footed runner had before he took the ball. Even as the ball was snapped, Flash saw Butch Hagan dump his man out of the way. Then he drove through the hole like a streak and hit the red-jerseyed Chadwick before he could even tuck the ball away!

He knocked Chadwick a dozen feet, the ball flying from his hands. Lew Young was in there fast and lit on the ball just as the pileup came.

They lined up and it was the Tigers' ball on the Bear thirty yard line. Flash got away and Saunders shot a pass to him. He took the ball running and saw Brogan cut in toward him. He angled across toward Brogan, deliberately closing up the distance, yet even as the big fullback hurled himself forward in a wicked tackle, Flash cross-stepped and shoved out a stiffarm that flattened Brogan's nose across his face, and then he was away.

Chadwick was coming, and drove into his pounding knees, clutched wildly, but his fingers slipped and he slid into the dirt on his face as Flash went over for a touchdown!

Simmons kicked the point and they trotted back to midfield. Krakoff took the ball on the kickoff but Higgins started fast and came down on Krakoff like a streak. He hit him high and Butch Hagan hit him low, and when they got up, Krakoff was still lying there. He got up, after a minute, and limped into position.

There was smeared blood on Brogan's face from his broken nose and the big fullback was mad. Chadwick was talking the game, trying to pull his team together.

They lost the ball on the forty yard line and Higgins recovered for the Tigers. They were rolling now and they knew it. Flash shot a bulletlike pass to Saunders and the redheaded young lawyer made fifteen yards before he was slammed to the ground by Chadwick.

Chadwick was the only man on the team who seemed to have kept his head. Wilson came in for Brogan and when they lined up, Butch Hagan went through that line like a baby tank and threw an angle block into Wilson that nearly broke both his legs! Wilson got up limping, and Butch looked at him. "How d'you like it, quitter?"

Wilson's face flushed, and he walked back into line. On the next play Hagan hit him again with another angle block, and Wilson's face was pale.

Flash rifled a long pass to Simmons and the former All-American end carried it ten yards before they dropped him. On the next play Higgins went through tackle for the score.

The Bears had gone to pieces now. Wilson was frankly scared. On every play his one urge seemed to be to get away from Butch Hagan. Krakoff and Brogan were out of the game, and the Tigers, playing straight, hard, but wickedly rough football, rolled down the field for their third straight score.

They lined up for the kickoff, and Flash

took it on his own thirty-five yard line, angled toward the sidelines and running like a madman hit the twenty yard line before he was downed. They lined up and Saunders went through center for six. On a single wing back Higgins made six more, and then Simmons took a pass from Flash and was finally downed on the five yard line. Then Flash crashed over for the final score, driving through with five men clinging to him.

And the whistle blew as they got up from the ground.

Flash walked slowly toward the dressing room, his face mud streaked and ugly. Pop was standing there, waiting for him.

"You saved my bacon, son," he said quietly. "I can't thank you enough!"

"Forget it," Moran said quietly, "it wasn't me. It was those friends of yours. And give Butch Hagan credit. He lined up six or eight of them himself, to say nothing of what he did on the field."

He turned to go, and Micky was standing there, her face pale and her eyes large. She lifted her chin and stepped toward him.

"Flash, I'm sorry. Pop never believed, but for a while, I did. He—Ken—made it sound so much like you'd done something crooked."

"It was him," Flash said quietly. "I'm sorry for your sake."

"I'm not," Micky looked up at him, her eyes wide and soft, "I'm not at all, Flash."

"But I thought—?"

"You thought I was in love with him? That I was going to marry him? That was all his idea, Flash. He never said anything to me about it, and I wouldn't have. I went with him because the man I really wanted never asked me."

"He must be an awful fool," Flash said grimly. "Why, I'd—!"

"You'd what, Flash? You better say it now, because I've been waiting!"

"You mean—?" Flash gulped. Then he moved in, but fast.

Lew Young stuck his head out of the door, then hastily withdrew it. "That Moran," he said, grinning, "may be slow getting an idea, but when he does—*Man, oh Man!*"

A NIGHT AT WAGON CAMP

No horses stood in the corral, no smoke rose from the chimney. Jake Molina slid his rifle from the boot and rode with it across his saddle.

The squat, unpainted shack, the open-faced shed, the pole corral, the stock tank filled with water piped from the spring . . . nothing had changed. It was bleak, lonely, and drought stricken as always. . . .

Molina dismounted, careful to keep his horse between himself and the house. Pike should have been here to meet him but there was no sign of life, anywhere.

The ranch had been abandoned ten years before, and looked it.

Rifle in hand he crossed to the house, pausing on the step to turn for one more careful yet uneasy glance.

The kitchen was empty but for a bare table, and a broken chair that lay on its side. Crossing to the fireplace he turned a charred stick with the muzzle of his rifle, then knelt and put his fingers upon it for an instant. It was cold and dead.

There were two more rooms. Using his rifle like an extension of his arm he pushed open the doors, but there was nothing but a dried-out, sunbaked boot, and a coat that had been dropped on the floor. There was no dust on the coat however, and it lay in a scuffle of recent footprints . . . in this abandoned place here was something that did not fit, something important to his quest.

Crossing to the coat he touched it with gentle fingers, and found a piece of board shoved down in the inside pocket. On it something had been scratched with a nail:

Just rode in, Lew Stebbins—
Monty Short—a stranger.

It was signed by Pike.

He stepped outside and looked slowly around. By now they would be miles from here, for they had not known he was coming. In growing fear he realized what they must have left behind. Grimly, he dropped the coat to his feet and slipped the thong off of his right-hand gun. He listened, and heard only the trickle of water, the wind, and an aimless tapping that came at intervals. The tapping drew him and he walked around the end of the corral toward the shed.

Pike was suspended by his wrists, arms spread wide and tied to poles of the shed wall. His chin hung down on his chest, and his toes just barely touched the earth. His shirt had been ripped from his body and his body had been beaten by a length of trace chain which now hung over the top bar of the corral. It was the wind, moving that chain in the hard gusts, that caused the tapping he had heard.

Pike had been dead for several hours, yet he had lived long enough. . . . With one toe he had scratched an arrow, pointing west.

Until he had met Pike, the trails Jake Molina had ridden were ridden alone, for it was his nature to ride alone, to ask nothing of any man but to be let alone. With Pike he had gone up the trail to Kansas, and he knew what Pike would have done for him, and what he must do for Pike. Above all there was Tom Gore's family to think of, and those neighbors who had trusted him with their cattle.

He buried Pike where the shack cast a shadow, and put a marker over the grave. Once, straightening up suddenly, he caught a flash of light from a hillside, and then he worked on and finished his job, sure he was being watched.

He rode out of the ranch yard at a lope and went up to the crest of the ridge, then went west holding to the skyline. Usually a bad thing to do, he did it now because the country lay wide and he'd rather see than worry about being seen. He headed due west, following the trail of the three riders until it broke off and went into the badlands to the south.

On the third morning he started early and when well down the trail he turned off and doubled back parallel to the route he had followed. He was back behind a clump of mesquite but had the trail fairly covered, and he waited no more than an hour.

Through the leaves he saw a man in a black suit coat and a black hat of more expensive make than a cowhand could afford. The man's face was wide and strongly boned, and although his saddle was worn from use, the boots had been well polished before the dust fell on them.

When the man had gone by Molina stepped into the trail. "You'd better have a good reason for following me, mister, and I'd better like the reason."

"I believe we should talk," the man said. "I think we're doing the same job."

Molina waited, never taking his eyes off the stranger.

"You buried a man back yonder, and you're trailing the three men who killed him. I want those men, too," the man continued.

"If you're the law you're not needed. If you're an outlaw you're trailing men who don't want company."

"I'm a Pinkerton man."

"Most places that would get you killed."

"My name is Hale. Do you know who you're following?"

"Pike told me."

Hale looked at him carefully. "Now that's interesting. Pike was dead before you got there because I was there before you were. He couldn't tell you anything."

Molina took the piece of shingle from his pocket, and explained how he found it.

"Pike was a shrewd man. He also knew me, and he knew how I think. He also knew that I know what they want, and somehow he thought things out so that when they lead me to the place, I'll be the one who finds it."

"Money?"

"Yes . . . it belongs to friends of ours."

Hale lit a cigar. "My job is to get those men and I can use help just as much as you can. Monty Short is a gunman, and Stebbins was a buffalo hunter, and is one of the best rifle shots around. I don't know the other man, but I've an idea. Why don't we ride together?"

"Up to you . . . I'm riding west. Come along if you've a mind to."

The country was broken into canyons now, the slopes covered with scattered juniper. Nor was the trail difficult to follow, for at no time had there been an effort to conceal it; the men had no reason to believe themselves followed.

"Nobody ever comes into this country," Molina said, "too dry for ranching these years, no more buffalo, so the Comanches rarely come. It's an empty land."

"Want to tell me about the money?"

"Tom Gore drove cattle belonging to some friends and himself to Dodge. He sold out for thirty thousand in gold and started home, and then he got the idea that some of his hands were going to rob him, so he gave a message to Pike telling him to take it to the ranch, and telling where the gold was, then he slipped out one night and hid the gold. When they murdered him for it a few nights later, they found nothing."

"And you know where it is?"

"Only Pike knew, so Pike had to tell them when he saw they were going to kill him, anyway. Otherwise nobody would ever know where it was . . . he's relying on me to trail them and find it before they do, failing that, to take it from them."

"A large order."

It was cold, with a chill wind blowing over the country and moaning in the canyons. The trail of the three riders had vanished. Hale studied the earth, but saw nothing. Molina did not slow his pace, nor did he pause to look around.

"You know where you're going?" Hale asked mildly.

"Sure . . . only three ways they can go

from out here. Everything in the desert that moves has to move toward a water hole. Over there," he pointed southeast, "are the Comanche Wells . . . seventy miles as the crow flies, and out of the way for Tom Gore, who was heading home.

"Gore was coming from the northwest, but he never got this far. So the Wells are out. That leaves Lost Lake and the Wagon Camp. They found Gore's body at Lost Lake, so my guess would be Wagon Camp or some dry camp near there."

"I see." Hale considered the subject. "What if they don't think the same way?"

"They will. They've got to. All life is tied to water holes here, and they know every camp because two of them, at least, rode with Gore when he was killed."

Molina drew up, studying the ground. He walked his horse forward a little, then drew up again. "That's funny. They're going to Lost Lake."

Hale lit a cigar and waited. He was out of his depth and realized it. He had believed himself a good tracker, yet he could see nothing here, no sign of passage more than a crow might have left. Molina rode on a few steps further, then returned.

"They're going to Lost Lake, so we'll cut across country to Wagon Camp."

"What if we lose them?"

"We won't."

They came up to Wagon Camp in the cool of the evening, and watered their horses at the seep and stood in the stillness looking around them. The wind ruffled the water in the pool, and Molina looked around carefully. A quail called in the shadows.

"We're here," Hale said, "or were you just guessing?"

"The gold will be here," Molina said. "I'm sure of it."

Squatting over a small fire built from gathered sticks and buffalo chips, Hale began to prepare their food. He was a big man and in his shirt sleeves the bulging muscles in his arms stretched his shirt. He wore suspenders and sleeve garters. Jake dipped water for coffee and gathered more fuel.

The Wagon Camp was only slightly less barren than the country around. Here where the water from the seep irrigated a small meadow and some bordering trees, there were two dozen scattered cottonwoods, several of them huge and ancient; there were some vines, willow brush, and further away, low-growing mesquite and prickly pear.

"We've got a day for sure," Molina said, "another day for possible. Then we can get set for trouble, because they'll be along."

Hale looked around doubtfully. "The gold could be buried anywhere," he said, "how would a man know? A few days of the blowing this country gets and it would look like any other place."

"He didn't bury it." Molina squatted on his heels and fed sticks into the fire. "He would have been afraid of the noise. He hid it someplace that was ready for him."

"Noise?"

"Digging . . . at night it would have awakened everybody. Even if he dug it out with his hands it would have to be a pretty fair-sized hole, and men on the trail sleep mighty light."

Yet by sundown the following day they were no closer to the solution. Every hole in the rocks behind the pool, and there were not many, had been examined. Trees, brush piles, everywhere either of them could imagine had been carefully checked. It could not have been far from camp, yet they looked and looked without luck.

Hale was irritable. "Molina, you've had it your way. Now we're here, and for all we know they've got your gold and have ridden out of the country. I say we mount up and ride out of here."

Molina glanced up. "You ride out. That gold is here, and sooner or later they'll come. Maybe tonight."

Hale got up and walked to his horse. He picked up his saddle to swing to his horse's back but when he looked across the saddle blanket he froze. "I see them," he said. "They're coming now, and they've seen our fire."

"Sit tight then, and be ready."

They came riding, spread out and ready for trouble. They drew up and Molina looked up and said, "Light and set. The coffee's hot."

"Where'd you come from?" Stebbins was doing the talking. Short was beside him, the stranger a little behind. He was a thin, narrow-faced man with empty eyes.

"Fort Griffin," Molina lied coolly, holding his cup in his left hand.

They did not like it, that was obvious

enough. They didn't like Hale sitting there with a shotgun across his lap, either.

These were the men who had tortured and killed Pike. Molina thought of that and grew hard and cold inside.

"You're off the trail, aren't you?" he asked. "This is one of the loneliest water holes in creation."

Monty Short got down from his horse. "I'll try that coffee," he said, and held out a cup for it.

Molina smiled at him. "There's the pot. Pour it for yourself."

Molina's words had apparently aroused the stranger's curiosity, and he sized Molina up with attentive eyes.

"You might be off the trail yourself," the stranger suggested. "This is, as you say, a lonely water hole."

"Used to be good country," Molina agreed, conversationally, "there was good grass all through here." He indicated Hale. "This man is Bob Hale; he's a cattle

buyer, and finances some ranching operations. We figured to start us a place right
here if the grass is good."

Stebbins chuckled without humor. "A
man's lucky to find feed for his horse. You
couldn't run ten head on ten square miles
of it now."

The stranger was still watching Molina
and suddenly he said, "I don't like him,
Lew," he indicated Molina, "this one is
smart."

All three looked at Molina, and ever so
gently Hale's shotgun moved so it was still
on his lap but pointed casually at the
group. The movement went unobserved
with all attention centered on Molina.

Molina lifted his coffee cup and sipped
a swallow of coffee, and then said quietly,
"So you don't like it. We got here first.
We're staying. If you boys want to use the
water, you're welcome."

"We think you're the ones who should
leave," Short spoke suddenly. "We think
you should mount up and ride out."

Molina smiled wryly. "Now that's fool-ish talk, Monty. You might get us but we'd take a couple of you with us, and probably all three. You and Lew aren't going to buy trouble you don't need."

Molina merely looked at them. "I told you . . . I came here from Fort Griffin, but I've also been in Mobeetie. What you do is your own business, but I wouldn't go back that way with posters on both of you."

Stebbins turned abruptly away, and as he did so, he saw the shotgun in Hale's hands. "Let's build a fire, Monty," he said, and he walked away. After an instant's hesitation, the others followed, the stranger lingering to take a last, careful look at Molina.

When they had gone, Molina sat down and filled his cup. "If I could only think!" he said angrily. "I know the stuff is here." Then he looked across his cup at Hale. "Which one are you after?"

"Short and Stebbins . . . train holdup.

They didn't get much, but that doesn't matter to us. That other one . . . he should be wanted somewhere."

It was after midnight, and Hale was on guard when they heard the wagon. Hale had been watching the other fire. He wanted his prisoners and expected to take them when they fell asleep, but they had a man on watch also, and there was small chance to even make a move without being seen. Then he heard the sound of wheels.

Hale did not believe what he heard, and neither did Stebbins, who was on watch in the other camp. Stebbins got to his feet and drew back from the fire, and Hale did likewise. Somehow the sound got through to Molina and he sat up.

The wagon rolled in from the darkness, drawn by two mules, and stopped on the edge of the firelight. There was a bearded man on the seat, and beside him a girl.

She was young; Molina saw that quickly . . . and her eyes found his across the intervening space with what seemed to be a plea for help. Yet that was foolish . . . he could not read a glance at that distance . . . but of one thing he was sure; she did not belong with the man on the wagon seat beside her.

When he got down and the firelight fell on his face, Molina saw the man was old, but still strong and wiry, and there was a sly, suspicious way about him that Molina distrusted.

"Quite a settlement," the old man looked around inquisitively, "somethin' goin' on?"

"Just passing through," Molina said. "How about you?"

The old man chuckled. "Might say we're passin' through, ourselves. My name's Barnes . . . that there's my niece, name of Ruth Crandall." He looked around carefully, his eyes remaining on the other fire for the longest time.

"Now there," he said, his eyes on the stranger, "is a man to remember."

"You know him?"

"Why sure. I'd say I know him . . . but he don't know me. Not yet, he don't." He threw a shrewd glance at Molina. "Name of Van Hagan . . . a man well known in Montana and Wyoming."

He peered around. "Been some time since folks camped around here, I expect." He paused. "Can't see how anybody would drive cattle through here."

"Nobody has," Molina told him, "lately."

"Now that's odd," Barnes spat, "for I did hear about a man named Gore driving through this country."

Molina took out the makings and began to build a smoke. Was everybody in Texas thinking about that gold? "Tom Gore," he said, "made his drive away east of here. He was driving for Wichita, then changed his mind and went to Dodge."

Barnes nodded. "Now that sounds

right. It surely does. Maybe it was when he was coming back that Gore went through here, and a passel of hands with him." He turned his head on his thin, buzzardlike neck. "Might you be one of them?"

"I worked for Tom on the home ranch," Molina said. "He was a friend of mine."

Ruth had gotten down from the wagon and walked nearer, and as they talked, she listened, looking from time to time at Molina, but trying to keep out of Barnes' line of sight. There was more here, Molina decided, than was apparent at first glance. One thing was obvious: here was another man on the trail of the Gore money.

It seemed impossible for anything to be hidden here, of all places. And he had looked around and examined the ground pretty thoroughly on the basis of earlier familiarity. However, Tom Gore had known this place, and so had Pike. Gore had planned to have Pike locate the gold and there might have been something each knew that was unknown to anyone else.

Obviously, the three outlaws did not know the exact location or they would have made a move toward it . . . or were they worried by Molina and Hale?

They had murdered once for this gold, and they would not hesitate again.

Hale stood guard and Molina slept while the camp quieted down, and in the early hours before dawn, he awakened Molina.

"All quiet . . . But I don't believe those boys will wait much longer."

Molina slid out of his bed roll and pulled on his boots. The night was cold, the coals of the fire glowed red with a few thin tendrils of flame licking the length of sticks just placed in the fire. Across the way the other fire was only a faint glow, and the wagon was silent. Molina could see Barnes bedded down beneath the wagon.

Moving back from the fire he saw Hale turn in and then he moved back still further until only his boots showed in the edge of light. Beyond that his figure was shrouded by the dead black of the shadow under a huge cottonwood. Carefully, he slid out of his boots and donned the moccasins he always carried folded in a pocket. Leaving the boots where they could be seen, the upper part of them in the shadow, he moved back away from the fire, and from among the trees he studied the camp with infinite care.

There were no hollow trees, no box concealed in a fork of the branches, and it had not been sunk in the pool at the seep. The water was shallow and perfectly clear. Nor were there any signs of digging . . . blown dust would have concealed it long since.

A thought caught at his attention, and

he scowled, trying to grasp what it was he had almost thought of but which had slipped his attention. And then he saw movement at the back of the wagon.

Ruth Crandall was getting out, ever so carefully, of the covered wagon.

He watched her get down from the wagon and fade back into the darkness. When he located her again it was by the faintest of sounds, and near him. He spoke in a whisper. "Late to go hunting."

She came up to him in the darkness. "Take me away from here, Mr. Molina. Just take me away."

"What's wrong? There is a problem with your uncle?"

"He's not my uncle! Not really. He married my aunt after my uncle died. Neither of them were related to me by blood. Then a few weeks ago she died and he started over here."

"Why did he come?"

"It was Art. You remember Art

Tomkins? He worked with you at Gore's? He returned with the bunch after the drive, and he was one of those who planned to kill Mr. Gore. Well, he did help kill him, and then Monty, Stebbins, and Van Hagan killed the others. Then they tried to kill Art. After they left, he was hurt and he stole a horse from a ranch and came to us. He remembered hearing some movement at night while at Wagon Camp, so he was sure the gold was hidden here. He died a few days after he got to us, and here we are."

Molina remembered Art. A lazy, down-on-his-luck cowhand who was always talking about the James boys.

"You've got to get me away from him," Ruth insisted. "If you don't . . . he's been telling me how much money I could make in Dodge or Fort Worth. How we could live real easy on the money I'd make." She caught his arm. "I don't want that kind of money, Mr. Molina."

"All right," he said, "but stay shy of us until this is settled."

She disappeared as quietly as she had come. She moved, he reflected, like an Indian . . . and fortunately, for that old man would be a light sleeper.

Sharply, he was aware of something else. He had watched the camp while Ruth talked to him, but there had been a time or two when his eyes were averted, and something had changed at the camp over there. One of the beds looked mighty slack.

Gray light was showing in the east, and he shifted position suddenly, nervously, realizing he had been still too long. And as he changed position he heard a voice behind him say, "Right there, Molina. Hold it right there."

With what had happened to Pike fresh in his mind, he threw himself to the side and rolled over in the darkness and came up, firing at the dart of flame before he heard the sound of the shot. He heard the hard impact of a bullet on flesh and dove forward as a bullet struck where he had been.

Farther off there was a sudden drum of gunshots. He held his fire, and glanced swiftly toward his camp.

Hale was gone.

The wagon was dark, but there was nobody under the wagon where reflected light had shown the long dark bundle of Barnes, sleeping.

Nearby Molina could hear the slow, heavy breathing of an injured man, but the fellow might be waiting for a shot and he dared not move. There were leaves and brush under the trees, and while he had not made any sound moving, the next step might not be so fortunate. Yet he had moccasins on . . . he put a foot out carefully as he straightened up, testing the ground. It was soft earth. Carefully, he let his weight down.

Then he saw the man who had tried to take him. He was down on the ground but he was still gripping a gun.

Squatting, he felt around on the ground and found a dead branch, fallen from one of the trees above. He straightened up but did not throw it. Instead, reaching off to one side with the branch, he made faint rustling sounds in the brush. Instantly the shot came and he fired in reply.

The camp was very still. Carefully, he worked his way to the man he had shot and picked up his pistol, then stripped the gun belt from the body and looped it over his shoulder after loading the extra pistol and tucking it in his belt.

Hale had vanished; so had Barnes. Nowhere was there a sign of anyone. It was so still he could hear the horses cropping grass.

It would soon be light, and what happened after that would settle things here. He had not found the gold, and he had no intention of leaving without it. One of the outlaws was down, but the other shooting he had dimly heard while he was fighting his own battle might mean anything or nothing.

Hale had vanished at the first shot, but was he alive? Or injured and lying hidden?

Molina moved to the shelter of a large tree, then lowered himself to the ground. His rifle was in camp and he would need it. Crawling, keeping to the shelter of the brush, which was sparse but in the darkness sufficient cover, he got back to a place close to their own fire. Only gray coals remained, a slow thread of smoke rising in the still air of the hour before dawn.

The sky in the east was gray with a shading of lemon near the horizon.

Nothing moved.

And then there was movement, the slightest stirring in the darkness near the rear wheel of the wagon, and a faint glint of light on a rifle barrel. Barnes was lying there with a rifle, probably the buffalo gun Molina had seen him with earlier. And on whose side was Barnes?

Neutral, Molina decided, neutral and protecting himself while the others fought it out, and then he would do his part. So there was that to consider during whatever took place now, and whoever won must be prepared to handle Barnes.

Dawn came slowly on the high plains, the sun rising behind far gray clouds. Barnes was discernible now, sitting at the rear wheel of the big wagon, his rifle ready for use, an armed spectator.

Ruth got down from the wagon and went to the fire. Adding fuel she built up the fire and put on a coffeepot. Then she went quietly about the business of preparing breakfast. Molina glanced at her from time to time, astonished at her coolness in the midst of a situation where shooting might break out again at any moment.

From where he lay he could cover the area at Wagon Camp. His only danger was if someone got behind a big clump of prickly pear off on his left and outside the grove of trees and brush. Some of that pear was tall as a man, and it was a big clump, banked with drifted sand. It made him uneasy, and he wanted to move, but there was no chance.

Desperately, he wanted his rifle, and he could see the stock from where he lay. Beyond it he could see a man's shoulder and hand. It was Hale.

The Pinkerton man lay in the slight hollow at the seep, a hollow just deep enough to give him the slightest cover, but whether he was alive or dead, Molina could not see.

Windblown sand had heaped up around some of the trees, but elsewhere the wind had scooped hollows, exposing the roots. No one of these places seemed adequate cover, and it was unbelievable that within this small area there should be four men hidden from each other.

Four men who waited for the slightest

move, four men ready to shoot and to
kill . . . and at one side, an old man with
a rifle, taking no part, but also ready to
kill. And a girl who prepared a meal in
the midst of it, who went about her task
as though the scene were as peaceful as it
actually appeared.

An hour went by, and the wind skit-
tered a few leaves along the ground,
stirred the green hands of the cottonwoods.

A storm was coming. . . .

Immediately, Jake Molina began to
think of how he could turn the storm to
advantage. He had been waiting for the
others to move . . . he would wait no
longer.

Hale had to have his prisoners, but all
Molina had to have was the gold. Too
many people needed that money, and although it would make none of them rich,
it would help them through the bad
times . . . especially the Gore family, who

would have no husband now, and no father.

And Hale might be dead . . . there had been no move from the shoulder he could see, or no move that he had observed.

Taking his Colt from its holster, Molina touched his tongue to dry lips and stood up. He might outflank and drive them into the open, for where they were hidden there was no more shelter than either he or Hale had.

He moved swiftly, dodging into a position behind another tree, and the shot that came was much too late . . . next time they would be prepared for him.

Ruth had merely glanced up from her fire. Barnes had shifted position enough so that he was on one knee ready for the final shot, when his chance came.

There was a big tree in the direction he was headed, not over fifteen feet away, but that was where they would expect

him to go. Straight ahead of him was another cottonwood, almost in line with his
present hiding place. He ducked around
his tree and ran and as a head and a rifle
came up he fired—fired as his right foot
hit ground. He saw the man jerk and
drop his rifle, drop from sight, and then a
hand came swiftly up to grab the rifle.

He was closer now, and he was out of
the trees except to his right or left.

He was sure the man in the hole had
not been wounded badly, probably only a
burn, or even more likely, just a bullet
passed his ear. But enough to make him
cautious about lifting his head.

No move from Hale, and none from
the second of the murderers, but Molina
was not fooled . . . the other man was
there, waiting.

It was point-blank range now, and no
chance to get to one of those trees to
right or left, but it was no more than sixty
feet to where the one man lay waiting.

He swung his eyes, peering past the tree, trying to find the second man.

Suddenly a voice called out, "Barnes! We'll split even if you get Molina!"

Barnes hesitated, and in that instant, Hale came up out of the basin by the pool, gun in hand. He took one quick step to the right and fired across the rocks behind the pool.

The man opposite Molina started to rise and Molina sprang from behind his tree and ran three quick steps toward him, slid to a halt and fired. The gunman had leaped up, but the bullet caught him in the shoulder and spun him halfway around.

Barnes lifted his rifle to fire and Ruth threw the coffeepot at him. It struck him alongside the head and ruined his aim. The buffalo gun went off into the air and Molina sprang into position half behind Monty Short where he could cover both the wounded Short and Barnes.

And that was the end of it.

Hale was walking toward them. "Van Hagan's out of it," he said. "Short, you're wanted for robbery. I'm a Pinkerton man."

Barnes got up slowly, holding the side of his head and moaning between agonized curses. The full coffeepot had not only scalded his face and shoulder, but the edge of the pot had cut his scalp and a thin trickle of blood ran down his face.

Ruth calmly picked up her coffeepot, refilled it and put it on the fire. Her face was white and her eyes large with fright, and she avoided looking toward Van Hagan, who was sprawled on the ground near the pool.

Molina walked over and picked up Barnes' rifle, then held out his hand for his six-shooter. Barnes hesitated, but Molina merely looked at him and, reluctantly, the old man drew his gun and extended it carefully.

"Drop it," Molina said, "I'll pick it up."

Hale was working to stop the blood in Short's shoulder. He glanced over at Molina. "Where's Stebbins?"

"Over there," Molina said, "but he isn't going anyplace."

Barnes got up slowly. "All right," he said, "we'll be pullin' out. You've no reason to hold me."

"You can go," Molina said. "Ruth stays with us."

Barnes' eyes flashed with anger. "She's comin' with me. She's my own niece. You got no call—"

"I am not your niece," Ruth said, "and I am going with them."

"You give us any trouble," Hale interrupted, "and we'll take you in for aiding and abetting. We might not make the charge stick but she'll go her own way nonetheless."

Barnes glared at them, then abruptly turned his back and went to get his horses.

Hagan and Stebbins were both dead.

With Monty Short handcuffed and Ruth ready to ride in on Stebbins' horse, Hale looked at Molina. "Looks like I've scored . . . what about the gold?"

Molina took the shovel from the wagon. "Why I'm going to get it now. Seems a man can be mighty slow to get things, sometimes. . . . Stands to reason, a man hiding something at night would have to drop it in a hole or cover it up. He couldn't be sure at night whether or not it could be seen, otherwise. Now there aren't any holes around, and if he did any digging the fresh dirt would be noticed even if the sound of digging wasn't. So what's the answer?"

"You tell me," Hale said.

"Why someplace where he could dig with his hands and where it wouldn't be noticed. That means drifted sand, to me."

Taking a shovel from the wagon he walked to the huge stand of prickly pear he had noticed before and walked around it until he found a place with an opening among the pear leaves and thorns that was large enough for a man to get a hand in without being badly scratched. The second shovel of sand disclosed the first of the sacks. In a few minutes he had them all.

Molina put the gold in his saddlebags and then saddled his horse. As he mounted up, Barnes walked toward them.

"What about my guns?" he protested.

"Tell you what," Molina said, "I'll leave them with the marshal in Fort Griffin. Anytime you want them you just ride in and explain to him how you lost them. You do that and you can have them back."

Ten miles and more than two hours later, Hale glanced over at Molina. "You should be a Pinkerton man. We could use you."

"Once I get this gold to Mrs. Gore," Molina replied, "I'll be hunting a job."

He glanced at Ruth. "Helen Gore," he said, "is a mighty fine woman. She could use a friend right now, and some help."

Where the trails forked at a clump of mesquite they drew up. "We'll be leaving you," Molina said. "Good luck."

Hale lifted a hand. "Come and see us," he said. "And thanks."

Monty Short, handcuffed, threw him a hard stare. "You get no thanks from me."

"You should," Molina said, "you're alive."

FLIGHT TO
THE NORTH

Turk Madden nosed the Grumman down gently and cut his motor, gliding in toward the dark waters of the cove. A dead stick landing on strange water in the middle of the night, and no flares to be chanced—it was asking for trouble.

True he had been assured by the Soviet Intelligence that it could be done, that the cove was wide enough and deep enough, and there were no dangers to navigation.

"If I get away with this," he muttered savagely, "anything can happen! And," he added grimly, "it probably will!"

It was bright moonlight, and he swung in toward the still waters of the cove with no noise save the wind-wash past the plane. The dark water lifted toward him, the amphibian hit lightly, then slid forward to a landing.

He would turn her around before the ship lost momentum. Then if anything happened . . .

The shore was dark; ominously still. If Powell and Arseniev were there they were to signal with a flashlight, but there was no signal. Madden hesitated, fuming inwardly. If he took off and left them, it would mean abandoning them to death. But if something had happened, if the plot had been discovered, then it would mean his own death to delay.

Suddenly he found himself wishing he was back in the East Indies running his airline in person instead of being up here in a lonely inlet on the coast of the Japanese island of Hokkaido waiting to pick up two secret agents.

From a single plane flown by himself, he had built his passenger, express, and freight service to three ships operating among the remote islands of the Indies. Then, wanting a change, he had taken a charter flight to Shanghai. From there he had flown for the British government to Vladivostok, only to be talked into flying down the coast of Japan to pick up Powell and Arseniev.

Arseniev he had known in China. He had been flying for Chiang Kai-shek when the OGPU agent had been working with Borodin and Galen.

He liked the Russian, and they had been through the mill together; so he accepted the offer.

Madden glanced shoreward again, tempted to take off. Then with a grunt of disgust he heaved his two-hundred-pound frame out of the pilot's seat, let go his anchor, and got his rubber boat into the water. "This is asking for it," he growled to himself, "but I can't leave while there's a chance they're still ashore. If the Japanese found them now, a firing squad would be the best they'd get."

The moonlight was deceiving, and the rocky shore was dark. Filled with misgiving, he paddled toward a narrow strip of beach. He made the boat fast to a log, and stepped out on the sand. Again he felt the urge to chuck the whole business, to get out while the getting was good. But he walked up the beach, stepping carefully.

It was too quiet, too still. Where were the men? Had they been captured? Had they merely failed to make it? Or were they here, without a light, unable to signal?

Loosening his gun in its holster, he stepped forward. He was rounding a boulder when he saw a shadow move. Instinctively, he crouched.

"Move," a cool voice said, "and I'll shoot."

Turk knew when to stand still and when to move. Now he stood still. A

dozen men materialized from the sur-
rounding shadows and closed in. Swiftly,
they took his gun and shoved him up the
trail between them.

"Well," he told himself, "this is it." The
Japanese had no compunctions about
their treatment of foreigners under any
circumstances, and spies—well, death
would be a break.

Ahead of him was a low shack, barely
discernible against a background of rocky
cliffs. A voice challenged, and one of the
Japanese replied, then a door opened, and
they were revealed in a stream of light.
Shoved rudely forward by his captors,
Turk Madden almost fell through the
door.

Two men were lying on the floor,
bound hand and foot. One was a slender,
broad-shouldered man with the face of a
poet. The other was short, powerful, his
face brick-red, his eyes frosty blue. The
latter grinned.

"Sorry, old man," he said, "we couldn't

make it. These blighters had us before we reached the cove."

Madden turned around, squinting his eyes against the glare. There were six Japanese in the room, aside from one with the attitude of an officer who sat at a table studying a chart. There was a coal oil light on the table beside him. None of the men were uniformed, or showed any distinguishing marks. All were armed with automatics and rifles. One carried a light machine gun. Their behavior, however, was definitely military.

The officer looked at Turk, his eyes narrow and heavy-lidded. "An American?" The Japanese smiled. "You sound like one. I am Colonel Kito Matasuro. I once lived in California."

"That makes us pals," Madden assured him, grinning. "I was a deckhand once on a San Pedro tugboat."

"But now I am a soldier and you are a spy," Matasuro murmured. "It is most unfortunate—most sad—but you must be shot."

He indicated Arseniev. "He will mean promotion for me. We have wanted him for some time. But like a shadow, he comes and goes. Now we have him. We catch three—we eliminate three."

Turk was acutely conscious of the flat hard butt of his .380 Colt automatic pressing against his stomach. It was inside his coat and shirt, but in his present predicament it might as well have been on the moon.

Despite the harsh realization that his time was only a matter of minutes at best, Turk found himself puzzling over the situation. Why were these men, obviously military, on this stretch of lonely coast in civilian clothes? Why were they here at all? Only a short time before it had been reported devoid of human life, but now there were signs of activity all about him.

Matasuro turned and rapped out orders.

"Sorry," he said, getting to his feet, "I would like to have talked to you of California. But duty calls—elsewhere."

With three of the men, he went out. From somewhere a motor roared into life, then another, and still another. A plane took off, and then the others followed. They sounded like pursuit jobs.

For a few minutes they stood in silence. Then Madden said, without looking around, "Fyodor, I'm taking a chance at the first break."

"Sure," the Russian said. "We're with you."

One of the Japanese soldiers stepped forward, lifting his rifle threateningly. He spoke angrily, in Japanese.

The door opened suddenly, and another Japanese came in. He was slim and wiry, his voice harsh. He merely glanced at the prisoners, then snapped orders at the three guards. Hurriedly, they cut the ropes that bound the ankles of the two Intelligence men, and jerked them to their feet. The officer and two soldiers walked out, and the guard behind shoved the prisoners into line and pointed to the door. Madden glanced quickly at Arseniev as the last of the men stepped out, leaving only the guard. "The table!" he snapped. Then he kicked the door shut with his foot, and lunging forward, struck the upright bar with his head. It fell neatly into the wide brackets.

Instantly, Arseniev kicked the table over and the light crashed and went out. Powell had wheeled and kicked the remaining guard viciously in the stomach. The man gasped, and fell forward, and the Britisher kicked him again, on the chin.

Turk, whose hands had not been tied, spun Arseniev around and stripped off the ropes that bound his wrists, then, as the Russian sprang to get the rifle, he did the same for Powell.

"Come on!" he hissed sharply, "we're going out of here."

Turk jerked the bar out of place and threw the door wide open. Outside, clear in the moonlight, stood the three Japanese, hesitating to shoot for fear of killing their comrade. Arseniev threw the rifle to his shoulder and fired, and they plunged outside. The officer had gone down, drilled through the face by the Russian's shot, but the other two jerked their rifles up, too late. Madden's automatic barked. Once . . . twice . . . One was down, the other fled, firing into the night.

"Get their guns, and let's go," Turk said. "My plane may still be okay."

Running, the three men got to the beach and shoved off in the rubber boat. The amphibian floated idly on the still water where he had left it, and they scrambled aboard.

Turk almost fell into the pilot's seat while Powell got the boat aboard, and the Russian heaved in the anchor.

The twin motors roared into life, and in

a minute the ship was in the air. Turk eased back on the stick and began reaching for altitude. Glancing back they could see the flat space of the landing field.

"How many planes took off?" Turk asked. "Did you hear?"

"Twelve," Arseniev said. He looked grave. "Where do they go? That is what I am thinking."

"It has to be Siberia," Turk said, at last. "If to China, why the disguise? If to my country, they would be bombers. Pursuit ships cannot reach Alaska from here."

"If they go to make war," Powell said, "they wouldn't be in mufti. There's more in this than meets the eye."

"Maybe," Turk suggested, "a secret base in Siberia from which they could strike farther west and south?"

Arseniev nodded. "Perhaps. And how many have gone before these? Maybe there are many. In the wilds of the taiga there are many places where hundreds of planes could be based."

"What's the taiga?" Powell asked.

"The forest that extends from the Urals to the Sea of Okhotsk, about twenty-five hundred miles from west to east, about seven or eight hundred north and south. I've been through part of it," Turk said; "looks dark and gloomy, but it's full of life. Miles and miles of virgin timber, lots of deer, bear, elk and tiger in there."

Turk leveled off at ten thousand feet, and laid a course for Vladivostok. His eyes roved over the instrument board, and he told himself again how lucky he was to have this ship. It was an experimental job, an improvement on the OA-9. No bigger, but much faster, with greater range, and capable of climbing to much greater heights. Also, it was armed like a fighting ship.

The men sitting behind him were silent. He knew what they were thinking. If Japan had a base far back in the great forest of Asiatic Russia, they could strike some terrible blows at Russia's rear while the Soviet was fighting a desperate battle with the invading Germans. It might well be the turning point of the war, and the three men—American, Russian, and British—had a like desire to see Germany defeated.

"You know Ussuria?" Turk asked Arseniev.

The Russian shrugged. "Who does, except in places? There are still wild lands along the ocean, and in the north. I am from the Ukraine, then Moscow, Leningrad, and Odessa. I have been all over Russia proper, but Siberia?" He shrugged once more.

Turk banked slightly, skirting the edge of a cloud. He was watching for the coastline. "I lived there a year when I was kid."

Powell looked at him in astonishment. "Aren't you a Yank?"

Madden grinned. "Sure, I was born in

Nevada. But when I was two my father went to the consul's office in Cairo. Then to Zanzibar, then to Tiflis in Georgia. My mother died in Zanzibar, and when I was eleven the revolution broke out. About the same time the old man died of pneumonia.

"Me, I lived around the towns of southern Russia, sleeping in haystacks and wagons, eating when I could. I lived a few months in the Urals, and then went to Siberia. I took up with an old hunter there, and lived and hunted with him for a year. He got killed, so I went south to Samarkand, and into India.

"I got back to the States when I was sixteen. Stayed two years, then went to sea. I've been back twice since."

Arseniev rubbed his chin thoughtfully. "You know a place? Where planes could land?"

Turk nodded. "I was thinking of it. Koreans used to hunt gold up in there. It might be some Japs came with them. It's a small lake almost due north of Lake Hanka and back up in the Shihote Alin Mountains."

"Want to try it?" Arseniev suggested. "We could refuel at Khabarovsk."

"Hell," Powell interrupted, "why get him into it? He's a commercial flier. You can't get paid enough for that kind of work, and taking a ship like this where it may get into unsupported action isn't sensible!"

"I agree," Turk said, grinning over his shoulder, "so we'll go. We'll land at Khabarovsk, refuel there, and you'd better tell them at Vladivostok what happened. Then we'll hop up there and look around."

In his mind, Turk went back over those Ussurian hills and forests, trying to locate the lake. He remembered those years well enough, and how he and the old Russian had hunted ginseng, trapped mink, and lived on the berries and game of the forest. They had gone west from the forks of the Nahtohu River, and come on the lonely little lake, scarcely a half-mile broad, and three-quarters of a mile long.

Leaving their plane at the field, the three men divided. Turk drifted down the streets, then found a quiet bar, and seated himself. He was eating a bowl of *kasha* and some cheese and black bread when three men sauntered in. They sat down near him, ordering vodka.

One was a huge man with a black beard, slanted Mongolian eyes and an ugly scar along his cheekbone. His nose had been broken, and when the man reached for his glass, Turk saw the man's hands were huge, and covered with black hair. The other two were more average looking, one short and fat, the other just a rather husky young man with a surly expression. The bearded man kept glaring at Madden.

He ignored it, and went on with his eating. Knowing his clothing set him off as a foreigner, Turk thought it was merely the usual curiosity. The big man talked loudly, and the three looked at Turk, laughing. Then the big man said something louder, still in Russian. Above the noise in the room Turk was unable to distinguish the words.

It was obvious they did not believe he understood Russian, and it began to be equally obvious that the big man was seeking to provoke a quarrel. The crowd in the bar did not like the big man, he could see, but he himself was a foreigner. Finally, above the rumble of voices, he heard the big man use the words "dumb" and "coward."

Turk looked up suddenly, and something in his glance stopped the voices. He spoke to the man serving drinks. "Vodka," he said, motioning to the gathering, "for those. For these—nothing."

There was momentary silence, and in the silence, Turk jerked a thumb at the big man, and said, contemptuously, "*Gnus!*" using the Russian word for abomination applied in the taiga to the swarms of mosquitoes, flies and midges that make life a curse.

The crowd roared with laughter. "*Gnus! Gnus!* Ha, that's a good one!"

His face swollen with anger, the big man got to his feet. Instantly, the crowd was still. From the expressions on their faces, Turk could see that most of them were frightened. Continuing to eat, he let his eyes slide over toward the men's table. There was an eager light in the eyes of the other two men, and Madden was sure this was what they had been working up to all evening.

The big man, whom he had heard called Batou, came toward him, and Turk continued to eat. When he was close by, the big man reached out suddenly. Turk's head slipped to one side to avoid the clutching hand, and then he kicked the big Russian viciously on the shin.

With a bellow of pain, Batou bent over, grabbing at his shin. Then Turk grabbed him by the beard with one hand, and jerking him forward, leaped to his feet and smashed a heavy right fist into Batou's midsection. The big fellow gasped and Turk shoved him so hard against the wall that he rebounded and collapsed to the floor.

There were audible gasps in the room, and then Madden quietly sat down and started to finish his cheese and *kasha*. Out of the corner of his eye he watched the two men at the table and Batou with apparent unconcern.

He finished his meal as the Russian got up. Stealthily, he observed the other man's rise. Batou's face was vicious as he strode across the room. "So!" he roared, "you t'ink it iss so easy to—"

Turk came up from the table, his left fist swinging.

The blow missed Batou's chin, slid along his face, and ripped his ear. With a cry of rage, Batou swung with both hands, but Turk went under them, and slammed both fists into the big man's stomach. Then he straightened up and grabbing Batou by the beard jerked his head forward into a driving left, and kicked his feet from under him.

Accustomed to winning fights by sheer size and strength, Batou was lost, helpless. He staggered to his feet, and in that instant, the other two men closed in. Adroitly, Turk sidestepped and kicked a chair in the taller man's path, then he struck the other man with a wicked pivot blow and caught him entirely unprepared and knocked him staggering into the wall. Turk closed in on the big fellow, jabbed a left to his mouth, then three more hard ones in rapid-fire order, hooked a hard right to the fellow's cheek and smashed his lips to pulp with a left hook.

He wheeled at a yell, and the younger man was on his feet, a knife poised to throw. Wide open and off balance, too far away to reach the man, Turk Madden was helpless. He didn't have a chance and he knew it. The man's hand moved back to throw, then there was a swish and a dull thud. Turk stared unbelieving.

The haft of a knife was protruding from the man's throat!

Turk spun about and Arseniev was standing in the door, another knife ready to throw. He smiled, lifting one eyebrow at Turk. "Turnabout is fair play, no? You save me, I save you. What is the trouble?"

Turk turned, just in time to see Batou and the other man slipping out the back door. He shrugged, letting them go. Briefly, he explained.

"I have heard some rumors," Arseniev said gravely, "that there is treachery here. This Batou. He is a bad man, a renegade. He murdered and robbed during the revolution. Then he went away to Korea. Now he is back here, and for no good. I believe this fight was deliberate."

They returned to the plane, and as they approached, Turk noticed three soldiers were on guard around the ship. Arseniev spoke to them briefly, the men saluted, and marched away. Powell was waiting inside the ship.

Turk slipped into the pilot's seat, and took the plane out on the field. There he turned into the wind, and in a few seconds they were aloft. Madden banked steeply, and flew west. Arseniev and Powell were surprised at the direction taken.

"If anyone's watching, that may keep them guessing awhile," he said, "even if not for long."

"If we find these planes, what then?" Powell asked.

Arseniev indicated the two-way radio. "We'll contact Khabarovsk, and they will send out a fleet of bombers. We'll show them a thing or two. Besides," he indicated the lockers, "we have a few messages for them ourselves, if necessary."

After flying a dozen miles due west, Turk swung the Grumman and started north, reaching for altitude. At twelve thousand feet he leveled off and soon left the hamlets and cultivated fields behind. He swung away from the railroad, and headed for the coast.

"I'll follow the coast to the Nahtohu, then follow it west to the forks. After that, finding the lake should not be hard."

He checked his guns. The Grumman mounted four machine guns forward; .30 calibers. Aft, there were three gun ports and two automatic rifles available.

"What have you been doing with this crate?" Powell demanded. "I thought you were flying express in the Indies?"

Turk grinned. "I was, but those East Indies are a long way from tamed yet. Lots of times I was flying gold, pearls, rubies, diamonds. Flying over wild country, over Moro, headhunter and cannibal country, and there's lots of renegades. Sometimes I had trouble."

Below them a cold gray sea was running up on the shore, boiling among worn black rocks, and curling back in angry white foam along the huge cliffs that lined the sea. The forest below them did not seem green, it seemed black, lonely and forlorn like the woods of a dead planet. Here and there on the heights there was snow, and down below in the occasional clearings they could see it too.

Turk studied the dead gray of the sky. "Storm making up," he said, "but there's plenty of time. That's the Nahtohu coming up." He swung the Grumman to cut over the woods and intersect the river trail.

"Madden!" Arseniev's voice was sharp. "A Nakajima fighter is coming down toward us!"

"Okay," Turk replied. "Get those automatic rifles and stand by aft. But don't shoot unless I give the word, or he starts. Then pour it into him!"

He flew right straight ahead. His mind was working swiftly. It would have to be quick, it would have to be surprise. The fighter's armament was no better, but his speed and maneuverability were much greater.

He glanced around. The fighter hadn't offered to open fire. It must be that he was uncertain. Turk slowed up suddenly to let the Nakajima overtake him. It did, coming at such a terrific rate that when the Grumman abruptly lost speed the fighting plane drew ahead. Madden suddenly banked steeply toward the Nakajima, and at the same instant, opened fire with his full forward armament.

The savage blast of fire caught the uncertain Japanese unprepared. A shell exploded against his instrument board, riddling his body with fragments. As he sprang up in the cockpit, a hurricane blast of machine-gun fire swept the ship from wing to tail assembly, and the Nakajima rolled over and started for earth, screaming like a dying eagle.

Turk pulled the ship into an Immelmann and wheeled back over the spot where the plane had been. But the pursuit ship was a gone gosling. It was headed for earth with a comet's tail of fire streaming out behind. Paralleling it fell the black body of the pilot, turning over and over in the air.

He'd had no chance to think, let alone to act.

"Nice work," Powell said, coming forward. His eyes were narrow, and he was sweating. "You don't gamble much, do you?"

Madden looked up quickly. "Gamble? With a war at stake?"

Powell laughed, his voice a little harsh. "Some would. You had me worried there for a minute!"

Turk eased back on the stick and began to climb. He glanced at the altimeter. Slowly the needle left ten thousand behind, then twelve . . . fifteen . . . sixteen. . . .

Powell looked uncomfortable, and loosened his collar. Arseniev, who had rejoined them, was watching Powell curiously.

At twenty thousand Turk leveled off and continued west. "What now?" Powell's breathing was heavy in the thin air. "Better land and look around on foot, hadn't we? If they see us we'll have a flock of pursuit jobs around us faster than we can think, and they'll do what you do, shoot first, then talk!"

"No," Turk said. "If they are down there, we're going to call Khabarovsk, then attack."

"Attacking twelve pursuit ships?" Powell said, his face getting red. "You're no combat pilot! You're mad!"

"Didn't you know that?" Turk grinned. "And that's not true, I flew in Spain."

Powell turned, looking at Madden. "You flew in Spain?"

"That's right," Turk nodded. "And I was a prisoner for a while during the siege of the Alcazar at Toledo. Remember?"

"Remember . . ." Suddenly, Powell's hand flashed for a gun, and Turk shoved the stick forward. The Grumman's nose dropped and Powell, overbalanced, plunged forward, his head smashing against the wall. He slumped in his safety belt, and Turk eased the stick back and brought the ship to an even keel. Arseniev's eyes were bright.

"All the time he was a traitor!" he whispered hoarsely. "All the time!"

"Sure," Madden agreed. "I couldn't place him at first. He's a German, lived in England for several years, but he was with Franco. You'd better tie him up."

Arseniev glanced down as Turk banked the ship. On the shores of a small lake were lined a long row of planes. Half of them were in the process of being camouflaged with branches and reeds. The others still were uncovered. There must have been a hundred.

Arseniev, his face white, bound Powell hand and foot, then he stepped over to the radio. "Calling Khabarovsk . . . calling Khabarovsk . . . enemy airdrome located . . . between the forks of the

Nahtohu . . . position 138 degrees east, 47 degrees 2 minutes north. . . . Approximately one hundred planes."

Turk glanced down again. Below them the airdrome was a scene of mad activity.

"Heard us!" he snapped. "Get set, I'm going down! Get on those bombs!"

Turk pulled the Grumman into as steep a dive as she would take and went roaring toward earth. When the ship was built she had been fitted with a bomb rack, and he had taken her just that way. Now it would come in handy.

Roaring toward the ground he saw one of the pursuit ships streaking along the field, and he opened up with the guns. The ship was just clearing the trees at the end of the field when it dipped suddenly, smashed into the timber and burst into flame.

The Grumman dove into the field so close that frightened Japanese scattered in every direction, then Arseniev pulled the bomb release, and Turk brought the ship out of the dive. For an instant he didn't think the wings would stay with her, but they did, and the ship was shooting away over the trees when the thunder of the bursting bombs reached their ears. He did a quick wingover and started back, his forward armament chattering wickedly.

He strafed the field from beginning to end, and a pursuit ship that had started to make the run for a takeoff spilled over into flame. He saw men start across the field.

Behind him, Arseniev was busy dropping incendiary bombs, then the Grumman began to climb, and Turk looked back over his shoulder. Several blazes were burning furiously around the field, two planes had definitely crashed there, and several were on fire.

He turned south. "We're getting out of here, Fyodor. Better inform your boys!"

Madden heard the voice replying behind him, then Arseniev switched off the radio.

"There's a force coming!" he yelled.

Turk tooled the Grumman on south, then swung away from the mountains toward the marshes. Suddenly the motor stuttered, coughed, and Turk worked, his face changing. The motor sputtered again, missed, then died.

"What is it?" Arseniev demanded.

"Gas!" Turk indicated his fuel gauges. "Must have winged us as we were leaving."

He put the Grumman into a slow glide, studying the earth below. It was marshland, with occasional ponds and lakes. But all were small. Suddenly, just ahead, he saw one that was somewhat larger. He pushed the stick forward, leveled off, and landed smoothly on the lake water. With what momentum remained, Turk tooled the ship into a small opening in the marsh. Nearby was a small island of firm ground.

"Better get on that radio and report," Turk said. "I'm going to look around."

He tried a hummock of grass near the plane, and it was solid. A flock of birds flew past, staying low. Turk turned to look at them, scowling. Then he looked up, studying the sky. There were clouds about, and the wind was picking up, but not much yet. Along the horizon there was a low black fog.

Suddenly, complete stillness fell over the marsh. Above, the clouds had ragged edges, and the black fog along the horizon suddenly lifted, and then the sun was covered.

"Arseniev!" Turk shouted. "Quick! We've got to get the ship lashed down. We're going to have a storm!"

In a mounting wind they labored desperately, furiously. There were no birds in sight now, and it was beginning to snow. When the ship was lashed down, Madden turned, wiping the sweat from his brow.

"Come on," he said. "We've got to make some shelter!"

"What about the ship?" Arseniev protested. "That will do, won't it?"

"Might be blown out on the lake. Start cutting reeds, and work like you've never worked before." Turk glanced around hastily. "Don't cut them there, or there. Just over there, and work fast!"

The wind was blowing in gusts now, cold as ice, and the snow was lifting into the air. Turk bent his back and slashed reeds with the bolo he always carried in the ship, sweat broke out on his face despite the cold, but he labored on, swinging with his bolo like a madman. Uncertain, Arseniev followed suit, not sure why they were cutting, but working desperately against time.

Leaping back to the bunches of reeds left uncut, Turk began binding them together with stout cord brought from the plane. Then he wove the long reeds closely together among the clumps, drawing them down low above the ground, and working the gathering snow close around the edges. Running to the plane, he caught up a canvas tarp and raced back, doubling it over on the ground under the covering of the reeds that was partly a hut, partly just a low shelter.

Suddenly there was a shout from Arseniev. Turk looked up, wondering. Powell had somehow broken his bonds, and had leaped from the plane. Turk went for his gun, but his hands, numbed by cold, fumbled, and before he could draw it the man had leaped to a hummock of grass, dodged behind a clump of reeds, and when they next saw him he was running at full tilt over the marsh. Once he fell waist deep in water, then scrambled out, and trotted on.

"Let him go," Turk said. "Maybe it's better than a firing squad, at that."

"What do you mean? You think—" Arseniev began.

Turk shrugged. "He's partly wet, he has

no shelter, no weapons. What do you think? He'll die before this night is out. Feel that wind, and imagine yourself wet—in that."

Arseniev shivered. "I can't." He looked around. "What now?"

"Crawl in between the canvas," Turk said. "I'll join you in a minute." He walked back and forth, piling the reeds over the canvas and feathering them against the wind. Then he trampled the snow down, and after a while, lifted the canvas and joined Arseniev.

The instant he was inside it felt warmer; over them they could hear the lonely snarl of the wind, and out on the lake the lashing of the waves, but over their covering of reeds the snow sifted down, gathering over them in a thick, warm blanket.

It was morning when he awakened. He turned over slowly, warm and comfortable. No wind was blowing, but he knew that it was cold outside. He touched Arseniev on the shoulder, then crawled out.

The world was white with snow everywhere. The lake was crusted with ice, and even the reeds bent heavily under the weight of the snow. The plane was almost covered with it.

"We've got to make a fire," Turk said, "and then uncover the ship. The way it is, a searching plane couldn't find us."

Sweeping the snow from a place on the ground, Turk went back to the shelter and brought out a handful of dry reeds. Arseniev collected some driftwood from the edge of the lake, and soon a fire was ablaze. Then they went to work, clearing the snow from the ship. It was a job, but it kept them warm.

Arseniev stopped once, looking over the white, empty expanse. "I wonder what his real name was?" he said.

"I don't know," Turk said. "I never heard."

It was an hour later when they heard the mutter of a plane. Soon it was circling above them, and then it leveled off and landed on solid earth not far away from the island where they'd spent the night.

Two men came running to them over the frozen marsh. "Marchenko!" Arseniev yelled. "It is good to see you, believe me!" The other man was Bochkarev, a flyer noted for his Polar exploits. They shook hands all around.

Two hours later, the Grumman was towed to solid earth and repaired. The big Russian ship took off, then the Grumman. Turk headed the ship south, toward Khabarovsk. They were flying low over the snow when Arseniev suddenly caught his arm.

Powell.

They knew him by the green scarf that trailed from his neck, a bright spot of color on a piece of ground swept clear by the driving wind. The man lay where he had fallen, frozen and still.

Turk Madden eased back on the stick and climbed higher. Ahead of them, the sky was blue, and the sun was coming out from the clouds. In the clear cold air the sound of the motors was pleasant, a drumming roar of strength and beauty.

TOO TOUGH
TO KILL

T he big truck coughed and roared
up the last few feet of the steep
grade and straightened out for the
run to Mercury. Pat Collins stared sleepily down the ribbon of asphalt that
stretched into the darkness beyond the
reach of the lights. Momentarily, he
glanced down at Ruth. She was sleeping
with her head on his shoulder. Even
Deek Peters, the deputy sheriff detailed
to guard him, had been lulled to sleep by
the droning of the heavy motor and the
warmth of the cab.

Pat shook himself, and succeeded in

opening his eyes wider. He had been going day and night for weeks it seemed.
The three-hundred-mile run to Millvale
and back was to be his last trip. Two weeks
off for his honeymoon, and then back at a
better job. Right now he and Ruth would
have been on the train headed west if it
hadn't been for that killing.

Why couldn't Augie Petrone have been
given the works somewhere else than
right in front of his truck as he left Mercury! Because of that they had detained
him several hours for questioning in
Millvale, and now, knowing him to be
the only witness, they had detailed Peters
to guard him. He wished Tony Calva and
Cokey Raiss would do their killing elsewhere next time. It had been them alright. He remembered them both from
the old days when he had often seen them
around, and had seen them both clearly
as they pumped shot after shot into
Petrone's body as his car lay jammed
against a fire hydrant. There had been an-

other man, too, a big gunman. He hadn't recognized him, but he would remember his face.

Suddenly a long black car shot by the truck and wheeled to a stop. Almost in the same instant, three men piled out into the road. Two of them had tommy guns. For an instant Pat hesitated upon the verge of wheeling the truck into them, full speed. Then he remembered Ruth there beside him, Ruth the girl he had just married but a few hours before. With a curse he slammed on the brake as Deek Peters suddenly came to life.

"Alright," Calva snarled, motioning with the .45 he carried ready. "Out of that cab! One wrong move an' I'll blast the guts out of you!"

Peters let out an oath, and whipped up his shotgun. The .45 barked viciously, and then again, and the deputy sheriff slumped from the seat to the pavement. Shakily, Pat helped Ruth down and they stood to one side. Her eyes were wide and dark, and she avoided looking at the tumbled body of the deputy.

"Well, would you look who's here!" Raiss grinned, stepping forward. "The smart boy who talks so much has brought his girlfriend along for us!"

"Alright, you two!" Calva snapped. "Crawl in that car and don't let's have a single yap out of you!"

Pat's face was white and tense. Reassuringly, he squeezed Ruth's hand, but his mouth felt dry, and he kept wetting his lips with his tongue. He knew Tony Calva and Cokey Raiss only too well. Both were killers. It was generally believed that Raiss had been the man behind the gun in most of the gang killings around Mercury in the past three years. Tony Calva was bodyguard for Dago John Fagan. There were two other men in the car, one sat at the wheel, and the other had stopped in the door, a tommy gun lying carelessly in the hollow of his arm.

Ruth got in, and the man with the tommy gun gave her a cool, thin-lipped smile that set the blood pounding in Pat's ears. The gun muzzle between his shoulders made him realize that there was still a chance. They hadn't killed him yet, and perhaps they wouldn't. As long as he was alive there was a chance of helping Ruth.

"You guys got me," he said suddenly. "Let my wife go, why don't you? She'll promise not to talk!"

"Fat chance!" Raiss sneered. "We've had too much experience with you talking. Why didn't you keep your trap shut? If you hadn't spouted off to those coppers in Millvale you might have picked up a couple of C's some night." He paused, and turned to stare at Ruth. "No, we'll keep the twist. She's a good-lookin' dame, and we boys may have to hide out somewhere. It gets kinda lonesome, you know."

Pat's muscles tightened, but he held himself still, watching for a chance. The car swung off down the paving in the direction from which he had come, and then, wheeling suddenly into a rutted side road. Sitting in the darkness of the car with a gun behind his ear, Pat tried to think, tried to remember.

The road they were on was one he hadn't traveled in years, but he did know that it led to the river. The river!

Suddenly, the car stopped. While the thin, white-faced gunman held a pistol to his head, he was forced from the car. Raiss was waiting for him, and Calva sat in the car watching Ruth like a cat watching a mouse.

They were on the bridge. Pat remembered the current was strong along here, and the river deep. There were four of them, and they all had guns. He might get one, but that wouldn't help. They might turn Ruth loose, they might just be talking that way to torture him.

"Don't shoot, Cokey," Calva said suddenly. "Just knock him in the head and let the river do it. There's a farm up here on the hill."

Suddenly, Ruth tried to leap from the car, but Calva caught her by the arm and jerked her back. Pat's face set grimly, but in that instant Raiss moved forward and brought the gun barrel down across his head in a vicious, sideswiping blow.

An arrow of pain shot through him, and he stumbled, and almost went down. He lurched toward Raiss, and the gunman hit him again, and again. Then suddenly he felt himself falling, and something else hit him. He toppled off the bridge, and the dark water closed over his head.

Hours later, it seemed, he opened his eyes. At first he was conscious of nothing but the throbbing pain in his head, the surging waves of pain that went all over him. Then slowly, he began to realize he was cold.

He struggled, and something tore

sharply at his arm. Then he realized where he was and what had happened. He was caught in a barbed-wire fence that extended across the river about three hundred yards below the bridge from which his body had been tumbled.

Cautiously, he unfastened his clothes from the wire, and clinging to the fence, worked his way to shore. He walked up the bank, and then tumbled and lay flat upon his face in the grass. For a long time he lay still, then he sat up slowly.

He had no idea of how much time had passed. It was still dark. They had, it seemed, tumbled him off the bridge for dead, not knowing about the fence. It was only a miracle that he hadn't gone down to stay before the barbs caught his clothing and held him above water.

Gingerly, he ran his fingers along his scalp. It tingled with the pain of his touch, and he realized it was badly cut. He groped his way to his feet, and started toward the road. He remembered the farm they had said was up above. Almost blind with pain, he staggered along the road, his head throbbing.

Ahead of him the fence opened, and he could see the black bulk of the farmhouse looming up through the night. Amid the fierce barking of a big shepherd dog, he lurched up to the door and pounded upon it.

It opened suddenly. Pat Collins looked up and found himself staring into the wide, sleepy eyes of an elderly farmer.

"Wha—what's goin' on here?" the farmer began. "What you mean—!"

"Listen," Pat broke in suddenly. "I'm Pat Collins. You call the sheriff at Mercury an' tell him Raiss an' Calva waylaid my truck an' knocked me in the head. Tell him they got my wife. Tell him I think they went to The Cedars."

The farmer, wide awake now, caught him by the arm as he lurched against the doorpost, "Come in here, Collins. You're bad hurt!"

Almost before he realized it the farmer's wife had put some coffee before him and he was drinking it in great gulps. It made him feel better.

"You got a car?" he demanded, as the farmer struggled to raise central. "I want to borrow a car."

The farmer's wife went into the next room and he hurriedly pulled on the dry clothes she had brought him.

"Please, I need help. You know me, I'm Pat Collins, and I drive for the Mercury Freighting Company, Dave Lyons will back me. If there's any damage to the car I'll pay."

The farmer turned from the telephone. "Mary, get this young man my pistol and those extra shells, an' get the car key out of my pants pocket." He paused, and rang the phone desperately. Then he looked back at Collins. "I know you, son, I seen you down about the markets many a time. We read in the paper today about you witnessin' that killin'. I reckon they published that story too soon!"

As the farmer's car roared to life, Pat could hear the man shouting into the phone, and knew he had reached Mercury and the sheriff. Coming up the hill from the river the memory of Dago John's old roadhouse at The Cedars had flashed across Pat's mind. A chance remark from one of the gunmen came to him now as he swung the coupe out on the road, and whirled off at top speed.

It had only been a short time since they had slugged him and dropped him in the river. They would be expecting no pursuit, no danger.

Two miles, three, four, five. Then he swung the car into a dark side road, and stopped. The lights had been turned off minutes before. Carefully, he checked the load in the old six-shooter, and with a dozen shells shaking loose in his pocket, he started down the road.

His head throbbed painfully, but he felt surprisingly able. It wasn't for nothing that he had played football, boxed, and wrestled all his life.

He reached the edge of the fence around the acres where stood the old roadhouse. The place had been deserted since prohibition days. Dago John had made this his headquarters at one time. Carefully, he crawled over the fence.

Pat Collins was crouched against the wall before he saw the car parked in the garage behind the building. The door had been left open, as though they hadn't contemplated staying. Through a thin edge of light at the bottom of a window he could see what went on inside.

Three men, Tony Calva, Cokey Raiss, and the white-faced gunman, were sitting at the table. Ruth was putting food on the table.

Pat drew back from the window, and

suddenly, his ear caught the tiniest sound as a foot scraped on gravel. He whirled just in time to see the dark shadow of a man loom up before him. He lashed out with a vicious right hand that slammed into the man's body, and he felt it give. Then Pat stepped in, crashing both hands to the chin in a pretty one-two that stretched the surprised gangster flat.

Quickly, Pat dropped astride him and slugged him on the chin as hard as he could lay them in. Afraid the sound had attracted attention, he crawled to his feet, scooping the gunman's automatic as he got up. He opened the door.

"Come on in, Red," the gunman said, without looking up, but Pat fired as he spoke, and the white-faced gangster froze in his chair.

With an oath, Calva dropped to the floor, shooting as he fell. A bullet ripped through Pat's shirt, and another snapped against the wall behind his head and whined away across the room. Pat started across the room. Suddenly he was mad, mad clear through. Both guns were spouting fire, and he could see Raiss was on his feet, shooting back.

Something struck Pat a vicious blow in the right shoulder, and his gun hand dropped to his side. But the left gun kept spouting fire, and Raiss sagged across the table, spilling the soup. Coolly, though his brain was afire, Pat fired again, and the body twitched. He turned drunkenly to see Calva lifting a tommy gun. Then Ruth suddenly stepped through the door and hurled a can of tomatoes that struck Calva on the hand.

Pat felt his knees give way, and he was on the floor, but Calva was lifting the tommy gun again. Pat fired, and the gangster sagged forward.

Collins lurched to his feet swaying dizzily. Far down the road he could hear the whine of police sirens, and he turned to stare at Ruth.

What he saw instead was the short

blocky gunman who had been in the car, the one that had shot down Petrone, and the gunman was looking at him with a twisted smile and had him covered.

They fired at the same instant, and even as he felt something pound his chest, he knew his own shot had missed. He lurched, but kept his feet, weaving. The heavyset man's face bobbed queerly, and he fired at it again. Then, coolly, Pat shoved a couple more shells into his pistol, hanging the gun in his limp right hand. He took the gun in his good left hand again, and then he saw that the other man was gone.

He stared, astonished at the disappearance, and then his eyes wavered down and he saw the man lying on the floor.

Suddenly the door burst open, and the police came pouring into the room.

•　　•　　•

When he regained consciousness he was lying on a hospital bed, and Ruth was sitting beside him.

"All right?" she whispered. He nodded and took her hand. Pat grinned sleepily.

MURPHY PLAYS
HIS HAND

Brad Murphy had been a prisoner in the box canyon for three months when he heard the yell.

He jerked erect so suddenly that he dropped his gold pan, spilling its contents. Whirling about, he saw the three horsemen on the rim and he ran toward the cliff, shouting and waving his arms.

One of the men dismounted and came to the edge of the ninety-foot precipice.

"What's the trouble?" he yelled.

"Can't get out!" Murphy yelled. "Slide wiped out the trail to the rim. I been a prisoner here for months!"

"Made a strike?" The man on the rim gestured toward the stream and the gold pan.

Instinct made Brad hesitate.

"No," he said cautiously. "Only a little color."

The man walked back and then he returned to the cliff edge, knotting together the ends of two riatas. While he was doing that, Brad Murphy walked back to the camp and picked up his rifle. On a sudden hunch he thrust his pistol inside his shirt and under his belt. Then he picked up the sack of dust and nuggets. It wasn't a large sack, but it weighed forty pounds.

When they got him to the rim, the man who had done the talking stared at the heavy sack, his eyes curious. He lifted his eyes to Brad's face, and the eyes were small, cruel, and sparkling with sardonic humor.

"My name's Butch Schaum," he said quietly. "What's yourn?"

"Murphy," Brad replied. "Brad Murphy."

The thin-faced man on the buckskin jerked his head up and turned toward Brad.

"You the Brad Murphy used to be in Cripple Creek?"

Brad nodded. "Yeah, I was there for a spell. You're Asa Moffitt." His eyes shifted to the third man on the paint. "And you'll be Dave Cornish."

"Know us all, do you?" Schaum said; his eyes flickered over Brad's height, taking in his great breadth of shoulder, the powerful hands. Then straying to the rifle.

Murphy shrugged. "Who doesn't know the Schaum gang? You've been ridin' these hills for several years." He rubbed his hands on his pants. "Any of you got a smoke?"

Schaum offered the makings. "Go on an' Dave can ride behind Asa," he said. "His horse'll carry double. I'll take the sack."

378 / Louis L'Amour

"No." Brad looked up and his green eyes were steady, hard. "I'll do that myself."

"Be too heavy on the hoss," Schaum declared.

"I'll carry the sack," Murphy replied, "and walk."

"Ain't necessary," Moffitt interrupted. "My hoss'll take the weight. It's only six miles to the shack."

Grimly Brad Murphy kept his rifle in his hands. They didn't know it was empty. They didn't know he had run out of the heavy .40-65 ammunition over two months ago.

Too much was known about Butcher Schaum. The man and his henchmen were cruel as Yaquis. They were killers, outlaws of the worst sort. Three years ago they had held up the bank in Silver City, killing the cashier and escaping with several thousand dollars. They killed one of the posse that followed them. In Tascosa, Dave Cornish had shot a man over a horse.

In Cripple Creek, where Brad Murphy had known Asa Moffitt, Asa was suspected of a series of robberies and killings. Escape from the canyon was now a case of out of the frying pan, into the fire. These men were not wondering what was in the sack; the only thing that could be that heavy was gold.

That gold would more than pay Brad for the three lonely months in the box canyon. It was gold enough to buy the ranch he wanted, and to stock it. His stake, the one he had sought for so long, was here. Now he and Ruth would have their own home. And a home for their son as well.

He suffered from no illusions. These men would kill him in an instant for his gold. They had delayed this long only because they had him, helpless, or practically so. Of course, there had been Asa's manner when he mentioned his name. Asa Moffitt knew about Brad Murphy. And Moffitt's queer reaction at the mention of his name had been a warning to Schaum.

"Ever have any more trouble with the Howells crowd?" Moffitt asked.

It was, Brad knew, a means of telling Schaum who he was. They would remember. His gunfight with the three Howells boys had made history.

"A little," he replied shortly. "Two cousins of theirs follered me to Tonopah."

"What happened?" Butcher Schaum demanded. Moffitt's question had told him at once who Murphy was.

"They trailed me to a water hole near the Dead Mountains. I planted 'em there."

Butcher Schaum felt a little chill go through him at the calm, easy way in which Brad Murphy spoke. Schaum was ruthless, coldblooded, and a killer. Moreover, he was fast enough. But he had never killed three men in one gun battle, nor even two.

For this reason, nobody was going to move carelessly around Murphy. After all, Murphy knew who Schaum was. He knew what to expect. Getting that gold wasn't going to be that simple. Getting it would mean killing Brad Murphy.

The shack was tucked in a cozy niche in the rocks. The level of the plateau broke off sharply, and under the lip of rock, the shack was built of rocks and crude mortar. It was not easy to approach, hard to get away from, and was built for defense. Any posse attacking the Schaum gang here could figure on losing some men. You couldn't come within fifty yards of it without being under cover of a rifle. And that approach was from only one direction.

They swung down, and Butcher noted

how carefully Brad kept them in front of him. He did it smoothly, bringing a grudging admiration to Butcher's eyes. This hombre was no fool. The sack never left his hand.

He followed them into the cabin.

"I'd like a horse," he said. "My wife and kid must think I'm dead. This is the longest I've been away."

"Too late to travel now," Cornish said. "That trail's plumb dangerous in the dark. We'll get a horse for you in the mornin'."

His rifle beside him, Brad sat at the table as Moffitt went about getting supper. The sack of gold lay on the floor at Brad's side.

"How do we know you won't tell the law where we're holed up?" Cornish demanded.

"You know better'n that," Murphy replied shortly. "You boys gave me a hand. I never—" he added coolly, "bother nobody that don't bother me."

It was a warning, flat, cold, plain as the rocky ridge that lined the distant sky. They took it, sitting very still. Moffitt put some beans and bacon on the table and several slabs of steak.

Brad Murphy had chosen a seat that kept his back to the wall. It had been a casual move, but one that brought a hard gleam to Asa Moffitt's eyes. His thin, cruel face betrayed no hint of what he was thinking, but he knew, even better than the others, what they were facing.

Idly, they gossiped about the range, but when the meal was over, Butcher looked up from under his thick black brows.

"How about some poker?" he asked. "Just to pass the time."

Cornish brought over a pack of cards and shuffled. Murphy cut, and they dealt. They played casually, almost carelessly. They had been playing for almost an hour, with luck seesawing back and forth, when Asa suddenly got up. "How about some coffee?" he said.

Brad had just drawn two cards, and he looked up only as Asa was putting Brad's rifle in the rack.

"I'll just set this rifle out of the way." he said, with a malicious gleam in his eye. "I reckon you won't be needin' it."

Schaum chuckled, deep in his throat. He won a small pot, and his eyes were bright and hungry as he looked at Brad Murphy.

"You fellows have played a lot of poker," Brad drawled. Coolly, he began rolling a smoke. "Ain't never wise to call unless you're pretty sure what the other feller's holdin'."

Cornish stared at him. "What do you mean by that?" he asked sharply.

"Me?" Brad looked surprised. "Nothin' but what I say. Only," he added, "it'd sure make a man feel mighty silly if he figured an hombre had a couple of deuces, then called and found him holdin' a full house."

Butcher Schaum's eyes were cautious. Somehow, Murphy was too confident, too sure of himself. Maybe it would be easier to get the gold by winning it over the table. He fumbled the cards in his big hands, then dealt.

Brad Murphy, his eyes half closed, heard the flick of the card as it slipped off the bottom of the deck. He smiled at Schaum, just smiled, and Butcher Schaum felt something turn over inside of him. He was a hard man, but in Murphy's place he would have been scared. He knew it. Only once he had been cornered like that, and he had been scared. Luckily, some friends arrived to save him. This hombre wasn't scared. He was cool, amused.

Schaum picked up his cards, glanced at them, and straightened in his chair, his face slowly going red under the deep tan.

The three kings he had slipped from the bottom of the deck, all marked by his thumbnail, had suddenly become deuces!

Trying to be casual, he turned a card in his hand. The mark was there!

He looked up, and Brad Murphy was smiling at him, smiling with a hard humor. Brad Murphy had dealt last. Obviously, he had detected the marks and added his own, to the deuces.

Suddenly, Butcher Schaum knew there was going to be a showdown. He wasn't going to wait. To the devil with it!

He tossed his cards onto the table. Brad Murphy looked up, surprised.

"Murphy." Schaum leaned over the table. "You figger to be a purty smart hombre. You know us boys ain't no lily-fingered cowpokes. We been owl-hootin' for a long time now. You got a lot of gold in that poke. We want a split."

Brad smiled. "I'm right grateful," he said, "for you pullin' me out of that canyon, and I wouldn't mind payin' you for a horse. But the future of this gold has already been accounted for, and I ain't makin' any sort of split."

He shifted a little in the seat, turning his body. One hand placed two double eagles on the table, taken from the pocket of his jeans. He then shifted his winnings from the game to the same pile. "Now, if you boys want to let me have the horse," he said, "I'll split the breeze out of here. Like I say, it's been a long time since I seen my wife and kid."

"You play a pretty good hand of poker," Schaum said, "but it's you that's bucking a full house. Asa's over there by the door. Yore rifle's gone. Cornish and me here, we figure we're in a good spot ourselves. It's three to one, and them ain't good odds for you."

"No," Brad admitted, "they ain't. Specially with Asa off on my side like that. The odds are right bad, I reckon. Almost," he added, "as bad as when the Howells boys tried me."

He smiled at Schaum. "There was three of them, too."

"Split your poke," Schaum said. "Ten pounds o' that for each of us. That's plenty of a stake."

"I'm not splittin' anything, Butcher," Murphy said quietly. "If you shorthorns want to be paid for draggin' me out of that hole, there it is." He gestured to what was on the table. "But I worked down in the heat and misery for this gold. I aim to keep it."

"We're holdin' the best hand, Brad," Schaum said. "So set back and make it easy on yourself. You divvy up, or we take it all."

"No," Murphy replied, "I'm holdin' the only hand, Butcher. You three got me cornered. You might get me, but that wouldn't help you—you'd be dead!"

"Huh? What do you mean?" Butcher sat up, his lips tight.

"Why, the six-shooter I'm holdin', Butch. She's restin' on my knee, pointin' about an inch under yore belt buckle." He tapped the underside of the table with the barrel.

He shoved back in his chair a little, then stood up, the Frontier Colt .45 balanced easily in his hand. "I'm takin' a horse, boys, an' I wouldn't figure on nothin' funny; this gun's mighty easy on the trigger."

Waving Asa around with the other two, he gathered his sack with his left hand and edged around the table toward the door. Slowly, he backed to the door, his gun covering them.

He stepped back. Butcher Schaum, his face swollen with fury, stared at him, his right hand on the table, fingers stretched like a claw, and stiff with rage.

He stepped back again, quickly this time. His foot hung. Too late he remembered the raised doorsill, he fell backward, grabbing at the air. Then a gun blasted and something struck him alongside the head. With his last flicker of consciousness, he hurled the sack of gold at the slope that reared itself alongside the cabin. It struck, gravel rattled, and he felt blackness close over him, soft, folding, deadening.

The first thing he realized was warmth. His back was warm. Then his eyes flickered open, blinding sunlight struck them, and they closed.

He was lying, his head turned sideways, sprawled facedown on the hard-packed earth outside the cabin door. It was daylight.

Butcher Schaum's voice broke into his growing realization. "Where'd he put that durned sack?" he snarled angrily. "My shot got him right outside the door, he didn't have no more'n two steps, an' now that gold is plumb gone."

"You sure he's dead?" Asa protested.

"Look at his head!" Cornish snapped.

"If he ain't dead he will be. I couldn't get no pulse last night. He's dead all right."

"Should we bury him?" Asa suggested. "I don't like to see him lying like that."

"Go ahead, if you want to," Schaum snarled. "I'm huntin' that gold. When I get it, I'm leavin'. You can stay if you want to. The buzzards'll take care of him. Leave him lay."

His head throbbing with pain, Brad lay still. How bad was he hurt? What was wrong with his head? It felt stiff and sore, and the pain was like a red-hot iron pressed against his skull.

Something crawled over his hand. His eyes flickered. An ant. Horror went through him. Ants! In a matter of minutes they'd be all over him. If there was an open wound—yet he dare not move. His gun? He had lost it in falling. No telling where it was now. If he tried to move they would kill him.

He could hear the three men moving as

they searched. Schaum began to curse viciously.

"Where could it get to?" he bellowed angrily. "He didn't go no more'n a few feet."

Other ants were coming now, crawling over his arm toward his head. He knew now that he was cut there. The bullet must have grazed his skull, ripping the scalp open and drenching him with blood, making it appear that he was shot through the head.

Piercing pain suddenly went through him. The ants had gone to work. He forced himself to lie still. His teeth gritted, and he lay, trying not to tense himself.

"I'll bet he throwed that sack down the gully," Cornish said suddenly. "It couldn't be no place else."

He could hear them then, cursing and sliding to get to the bottom of the gully that curved close to the cabin from the left. The bank against which he had thrown the sack was to the right.

Two of them gone. The ants were all over him now, and he could not stand the agony much longer. It was turning his head into a searing sheet of white-hot pain.

Where was Moffitt? He could hear no sound. Then, as he was about to move, he heard a step, so soft he could scarcely detect it. Then another step, and Asa Moffitt was bending over him.

"In his shirt," Moffitt muttered. "Where the gun was!"

Moffitt caught him by the coat and jerked him over on his back. "Ants gittin' him," he muttered. "Too bad he ain't alive." Asa knelt over him, and pulled his shirt open, cursing when he saw no sack. Then he thrust a hand into Brad's pants pocket.

It was the instant Brad had waited for. He exploded into action. A fist caught Asa on the head and knocked him sprawling. Lunging to his feet, Brad jumped for the man, slugging him twice before he could get to a standing position, and then as Asa grabbed at him, Brad jerked his knee into the outlaw's face.

Asa cried out sharply, falling over on his back, and Brad stooped over him, slugging him again as the man continued to yell, then he jerked Asa's gun from his holster and wheeling, ran for the rim of the gully.

His own gun lay nearby, and then he saw the standing horse. Grabbing up his own gun, he raced for the horse.

A shot rang out, and he saw Cornish come lunging over the rim of the gully. He tried a shot, saw that he'd missed. Realizing all chance of escape was gone, he ran for the house. Another gun roared, and then he plunged through the door and slammed it shut. Panting, he dropped the bar into place.

Outside he could hear shouts of anger, and Butcher Schaum fired at the door. From beside a window he snapped a hasty shot at Schaum, and smiled grimly as the man sprang for cover.

There was a tin pan filled with water near the door and he ducked his head into it, rinsing out his hair and washing the wound. From time to time he took a glimpse from the window. Obviously, there was a council of war going on down on the edge of the gully.

Freeing himself of some of the ants, he reloaded his pistol. A rifle stood by the door, and he picked it up. Digging around he found some .44-.40s and shoved cartridges into the magazine.

Hastily, he took stock. He had enough grub here for days. He had ammunition enough. They would know that as well as he. From the front the place was almost invulnerable. He glanced up, and his face tightened. The roof was made of rough planking and piled over with straw thatch. Fire dropped from the shelving cliff behind could burn him out.

How long would it take them to think of that? They wouldn't leave without the gold, he knew. And regardless of where it had gotten to, he wasn't leaving without it either.

The bank was in view of the window. He could cover it. The fact remained that they would never let him get away alive, and it would not take them long to resign themselves to burning him out. Much of their own gear was inside, which would cause some hesitation. It would be a last resort for them—but the end of him.

His only way out would be straight ahead, across that fifty yards of open space. Not more than one would go to the shelf above, and the other two would be waiting to cut him down.

Not more than one? His eyes narrowed. Was there a way to the top of the cliff? Hastily, he took a glance outside, caught a bit of movement in the brush, and put two quick shots into it with his rifle. Then he tried two more shots, spaced at random along the edge of the gully, merely as a warning.

Reloading the rifle, he went to the back of the cabin. The back wall was the cliff itself. Trying to recall the looks of the place, he remembered there had been some vines or brush suspended from the shelf. Perhaps he could get up under the edge of those vines! Taking a hasty glance through the window, he went to the back of the house.

There was a place where a plank was too short. Standing atop a chair, he began pulling at the thatch. It was well placed, and his fingers were soon raw from tugging at it, yet he was making progress.

From time to time he returned to the window. Several times, shots came into the cabin.

"Give yourself up, Murphy, and we'll split that gold anyway you want it," Schaum yelled.

"You go to blazes!" he roared back. He was seething with anger. "It's you or me now, so don't try none of your tricks! I ain't leavin' here now until all three of you are dead or my prisoners. Unless you want to hightail it out of here, I'm gittin' you, Schaum!"

A volley of rifle shots was the reply. He crouched below the stone sill, and when the volley ended, he tried a quick shot. A reply burned his shoulder, and he shot again, then put down the rifle and returned to his digging at the thatch.

Soon he had a hole he could peer up through. A wild grapevine hung down from the brush overhead, trailing down from the bending branches of the brush. Up in back of it was a hollow in the rock. It might offer a foothold. The hollow was right under the very shelf of rock he had seen on nearing the cabin. It would be invisible from in front of the cabin if he could get up behind that brush. There would be an instant when he would be half revealed. The instant when he reached up to get his hands on the brush or rock.

The day wore on, and he dug up some biscuits and munched them cheerfully. He found a couple of cartridge belts and slung them to his hips, holstering the guns. Then he stuffed his pockets with rifle shells.

"Gettin' hungry out there?" he yelled. "I got lots of chow!"

A string of vile curses replied to him, and he studied the terrain ahead of him through the crack of the door. A dozen bullet holes let little swords of light into the shadows inside.

He went to the bucket and drank, then he stripped and brushed more ants from him. Dressing again, he glanced from the window. The saddled horse was gone. As he listened, he heard the sounds of a rapidly ridden horse leaving. Then a shout from Schaum.

"Yore last chance, Murphy!" Schaum

shouted. "Come out or we burn you out."

He did not want them to think that he had planned for that. He fired two quick shots from the window, and drew one shot in reply. Then he heard something hit the roof. Hastily, he got up on the chair. Smoke came to his nostrils. He thrust his head up and got a whiff of smoke, then a blast of flame and heat! Thrusting his rifle through the hole, he struggled to pull himself up.

He got his shoulders through, then his six-guns hung. The thatch in front was roaring now and the fire was spreading toward him. Wildly, he ripped at it to make the hole larger. Then, getting a hand in a rock crevice, he tugged himself up.

The rock crumbled in his fingers, and with a wild gasp of despair he felt himself sliding back. Desperately, his hand shot out, caught a handful of brush. His arms jerked in their sockets, and then, slowly, he dragged himself up.

With his feet clinging precariously to a tiny ledge, he glanced back. His rifle lay where he had left it and as the fire spread across the roof the shells in the magazine began to explode . . . he heard yelling, what they thought was going on he couldn't imagine, maybe they thought he was still shooting at them. Hand over hand, he pulled himself up into the hollow under the shelf.

The roof below was a roaring furnace now. The slightest slip would send him plunging into the flames. Smoke rose in a stifling cloud. He pulled himself higher until the shelf was directly over his back. As he clung there, fighting for breath, he heard footsteps grate on the rock only a few inches over his head.

There would be no chance to get over the edge of the shelf as long as that man remained there. Clinging to the brush, his feet resting on a small ledge, only a couple of inches wide, he turned his head. A black hole gaped in the stone face. A hole scarcely large enough for a man's body, a hole under the shelf of rock.

Carefully, taking his whole weight on his arms, he lifted his feet and thrust them into the hole. Catching his toes behind a minor projection of rock, he drew himself back inside.

Dropping his feet, he felt around. Inside the opening, the hole was several feet deep. He drew back until he was on his knees, only his head in the opening. Less smoke was coming toward him now. He could hear shouts from below, and one from above him.

"See him?" The voice was that of Cornish.

"Blamed fool burned to death," Schaum said in astonishment. "He never even showed."

"I'm coming down!" Cornish shouted.

"You stay there," Schaum bellowed. "I don't like the look of this!"

Brad felt of the walls and top of the hole he was in. At the back it slanted down and around. But feeling at the top in back, he felt earth and roots. It was probably not more than two feet to the surface there, or very little more.

Where was Cornish? The question was answered when he heard the man shout another question at Schaum. He was probably at least thirty feet away.

Removing a spur, Brad Murphy dug at the earth. He worked carefully, avoiding sound. He dug at the soft earth, letting it fall to the bottom of the hole. Much of it fell on his own legs, cushioning the little sound. He had worked but a few minutes when taking a small root, he pulled down, a tiny hole appeared, and earth cascaded around him. Pistol ready, he waited for an instant to see if Cornish had heard him. There was no sound or movement, and he tugged at another root. More dirt cascaded around him. That time there was a muffled gasp and he heard pounding feet.

His gun was ready and it was all that saved him. Dave Cornish, his eyes wide and frightened, was staring down into the hole at him, gun in hand.

The man was petrified by astonishment. The man they thought had burned in the cabin below was coming up through the earth. Before Cornish could realize what was truly happening, Brad acted. The gun was ready. He shoved it up, and even as Cornish started from his shock, the six-gun bellowed.

The close confines of the hole made a terrific blast, and acrid fumes cut at Murphy's nostrils. Cornish fell forward, and bracing his shoulders against the earth atop the hole, Brad shoved himself through. He scrambled out, rolling over flat.

•   •   •

One look at Dave Cornish was enough. The man was dead. He had been shot right through the heart. Excited shouts came from below. The shot, muffled by the earth, had reached them but dimly. Yet they were alarmed.

"Butcher!" Murphy yelled.

Schaum was walking toward the smoldering cabin, Moffitt a few feet behind him.

Butcher Schaum froze, terror had turned his face to an ugly mask as he raised his eyes.

He dropped a hand for a gun, and Brad Murphy whipped up his own. Shots stabbed into the hot still air, something struck his shoulder, and he staggered one step, then fired. Schaum swayed drunkenly, tried to get a gun up, and then Brad fired again.

Behind him, Asa Moffitt swept up a pistol and emptied it in a terror-stricken blast of fire. Then he turned and ran for the gully.

Remorselessly, Brad Murphy waited an instant, then fired. Once, twice! The outlaw and murderer fell, rolled over, and lay sprawled out on the lip of the gully.

Calmly, Brad Murphy reloaded. He found the paint horse standing not far away, and mounting, rode down to the smoldering ruins.

A few minutes of search and he found his gold. The bag had hit and slid down the bank. It was lying there covered partially by dirt, visible but not likely to attract attention.

Shaking his head, he swung into the saddle and turned the horse toward town.

"Horse," he said, "you're takin' me home. I got to buy me a ranch for Ruth and my boy. . . . I reckon," he added, "they'll be right glad to see me."

He turned the horse down the trail. The nearest town was thirty miles away. Behind him the smoke lifted slowly toward the sky where a buzzard circled lazily in the wavering heat. Gravel rattled, and the horse felt good between Brad's legs, and he liked the heavy feeling of the gold.

AFTERWORD BY
BEAU L'AMOUR

Last year at this time I thought that *With These Hands* would be our last collection of short fiction. I knew that there were a few stragglers, but as we did a careful inventory of what had been published we discovered more and more stories. Finally, we realized there were enough for one more collection. So here they are, both Louis's first and last short stories, "Anything for a Pal" and "The Moon of the Trees Broken by Snow," as well as a pair of WWII adventures, four westerns, a couple of football stories, and two crime tales. As far as I can tell, "From the

Listening Hills," and my favorite, "Sand Trap," have never before been published.

I write this afterword with a strange mixture of feelings. We've brought you a great many new, hard to find, and sometimes fragmentary stories in the fifteen years since Louis's death. In many ways I've enjoyed the process, yet at the same time I'm glad that it is nearing an end.

Is this the last new Louis L'Amour book? I don't know. Are there more things we could publish? Yes, but I don't know if, or exactly how, we should. The future will decide these and other questions.

There is always more to be found at our web site, *louislamour.com*, where we offer a world of information, discussion forums, and photographs. For more of Louis's writings, you can take a look at *louislamourslosttreasures.com*. At the *Lost Treasures* site we are collecting articles, story outlines, incomplete short stories and novels, letters, journals, and notes covering everything from the innermost details of his most popular stories to his most outlandish and unmarketable ideas. Whenever possible I have added notes to bring this wide array of material into perspective. Also, our series of radio dramas can be heard on XM Satellite Radio, Armed Forces Radio, Cable Network Radio, and a selection of local stations that are posted on *louislamour.com*.

I want to take this final opportunity in print to thank some of the people who have helped us bring all of these stories to you and have helped me so much in sorting out the material for the Louis L'Amour Biography Project. First would be Paul O'Dell, who has assisted with everything from helping out after my father's death to running our website and editing our radio shows; Jeanne Brown, who keeps the biography project from dissolving into chaos; Daphne Ashbrook, who just joined us in information processing; Howard Gale, our recording engineer; and Charles Van Eman, who has written audio adaptations and been our ace bloodhound on the biography. Of course, we never could have done any of it without my mother, Katherine L'Amour, and her assistant, Sonndra May.

Earlier generations of helpers include my sister, Angelique, Katherine and Gavin Doughtie, Mara Purl, Helen Swart, Trish Mahoney, Paula Bayers, John Barrymore III, Cathy Sandrich, Jordan Ladd, and Lynn Adams.

The team at Bantam Books has been a powerfully creative force behind Louis's books since his death. We would like to thank everyone who has worked at Bantam for their continuing vision and hard work. Chief Executive Officers: Peter Olson, Erik Engstrom, Jack Hoeft, Alberto Vitale, Lou Wolfe, Oscar Dystel. Publishers: Irwyn Applebaum, Linda Grey, Marc Jaffe. Editors: Andrea Nicolay, Mike Shohl, Pat LoBrutto, Tom Dupree, Stuart Applebaum, Irwyn

Applebaum, Marc Jaffe, Saul David. Art Directors: Jim Plumeri, Yook Louie, Len Leone. Publicity: Stuart Applebaum, Barb Burg, Chris Artis. Sales: Don Weisberg, George Fisher, Cynthia Lasky. Audio: Jenny Frost, Robert Allen, Orli Moscowitz, Christine McNamara, Helena Terbush, David Rapkin, Charles Potter. Corporate Development and New Media: Richard Sarnoff. Marketing: Betsy Hulsebosch. Royalties: Pauline James. Inventory Management: Ken Graff. Subsidiary Rights: Amanda Mecke, Sharon Swados. Legal Counsel: Heather Florence, Harriette Dorsen, Matthew Martin, Paula Brian, David Sanford. Continuity: Lisa Faith Phillips, Vladimir Damianov. Remainders: Kathy Garcia. Special Sales: Pam Romano, Anne Somlyo, Maureen Cosgrove.

Thank you all; readers, and workers in research and publishing both.

Beau L'Amour

ABOUT
LOUIS L'AMOUR

"I think of myself in the oral tradition—as a troubadour, a village tale-teller, the man in the shadows of the campfire. That's the way I'd like to be remembered—as a storyteller. A good storyteller."

It is doubtful that any author could be as at home in the world re-created in his novels as Louis Dearborn L'Amour. Not only could he physically fill the boots of the rugged characters he wrote about, but he literally "walked the land my characters walk." His personal experiences as well as his lifelong devotion to historical research combined to give Mr. L'Amour the unique knowledge and understanding of people, events, and the challenge of the American frontier that became the hallmarks of his popularity.

Of French-Irish descent, Mr. L'Amour could trace his own family in North America back to the early 1600s and follow their steady progression westward, "always on the frontier." As a boy growing up in Jamestown, North Dakota, he absorbed all he could about his family's frontier heritage, including the story of his great-grandfather who was scalped by Sioux warriors.

Spurred by an eager curiosity and desire to broaden his horizons, Mr. L'Amour left home at the age of fifteen and enjoyed a wide variety of jobs, including seaman, lumberjack, elephant handler, skinner of dead cattle, and miner, and was an officer in the transportation corps during World War II. During his "yondering" days he also circled the world on a freighter, sailed a dhow on the Red Sea, was shipwrecked in the West Indies and stranded in the Mojave Desert. He won fifty-one of fifty-nine fights as a professional boxer and worked as a journalist and lecturer. He was a voracious reader and collector of rare books. His personal library contained 17,000 volumes.

Mr. L'Amour "wanted to write almost from the time I could talk." After developing a widespread following for his many frontier and adventure stories written for fiction magazines, Mr. L'Amour published his first full-length novel, *Hondo*, in the United States in 1953. Every one of his more than 120 books is in print; there are more than 270 million copies of his books in print worldwide, making him one of the bestselling authors in modern literary history. His books have been translated into twenty languages, and more than forty-five of his novels and stories have been made into feature films and television movies.

His hardcover bestsellers include *The Lonesome Gods, The Walking Drum* (his twelfth-century historical novel), *Jubal Sackett, Last of the Breed*, and *The Haunted Mesa*. His memoir, *Education of a Wandering Man*, was a leading bestseller in 1989. Audio dramatizations and adaptations of many L'Amour stories are available on cassette tapes from Bantam Audio Publishing.

The recipient of many great honors and awards, in 1983 Mr. L'Amour became the first novelist ever to be awarded the Congressional Gold Medal by the United States Congress in honor of his life's work. In 1984 he was also awarded the Medal of Freedom by President Reagan.

Louis L'Amour died on June 10, 1988. His wife, Kathy, and their two children, Beau and Angelique, carry the L'Amour publishing tradition forward.